Building Billions - Part 3

Building Billions, Volume 3

Lexy Timms

Published by Dark Shadow Publishing, 2018.

This is a work of fiction. Similarities to real people, places, or events are entirely coincidental.

BUILDING BILLIONS - PART 3

First edition. April 9, 2018.

Copyright © 2018 Lexy Timms.

Written by Lexy Timms.

Also by Lexy Timms

A Chance at Forever Series
Forever Perfect
Forever Desired
Forever Together

Alpha Bad Boy Motorcycle Club Triology
Alpha Biker
Alpha Revenge
Alpha Outlaw
Alpha Purpose

BBW Romance Series
Capturing Her Beauty
Pursuing Her Dreams
Tracing Her Curves

Beating the Biker Series
Making Her His

Making the Break
Making of Them

Billionaire Holiday Romance Series
Driving Home for Christmas
The Valentine Getaway
Cruising Love

Billionaire in Disguise Series
Facade
Illusion
Charade

Billionaire Secrets Series
The Secret
Freedom
Courage
Trust

Building Billions
Building Billions - Part 1
Building Billions - Part 2
Building Billions - Part 3

Conquering Warrior Series
Ruthless

Diamond in the Rough Anthology
Billionaire Rock
Billionaire Rock - part 2

Dominating PA Series
Her Personal Assistant - Part 1
Her Personal Assistant Box Set

Fake Billionaire Series
Faking It
Temporary CEO
Caught in the Act
Never Tell A Lie
Fake Christmas

Firehouse Romance Series
Caught in Flames
Burning With Desire
Craving the Heat
Firehouse Romance Complete Collection

Fortune Riders MC Series
Billionaire Biker
Billionaire Ransom
Billionaire Misery

Fragile Series
Fragile Touch
Fragile Kiss
Fragile Love

Hades' Spawn Motorcycle Club
One You Can't Forget
One That Got Away
One That Came Back
One You Never Leave
One Christmas Night
Hades' Spawn MC Complete Series

Hard Rocked Series
Rhyme

Heart of Stone Series
The Protector
The Guardian

The Warrior

Heart of the Battle Series
Celtic Viking
Celtic Rune
Celtic Mann
Heart of the Battle Series Box Set

Heistdom Series
Master Thief

Just About Series
About Love
About Truth
About Forever

Love You Series
Love Life
Need Love
My Love

Managing the Bosses Series
The Boss
The Boss Too

Who's the Boss Now
Love the Boss
I Do the Boss
Wife to the Boss
Employed by the Boss
Brother to the Boss
Senior Advisor to the Boss
Forever the Boss
Christmas With the Boss
Gift for the Boss - Novella 3.5

Moment in Time
Highlander's Bride
Victorian Bride
Modern Day Bride
A Royal Bride
Forever the Bride

Outside the Octagon
Submit

Reverse Harem Series
Primals

RIP Series
Track the Ripper

Hunt the Ripper
Pursue the Ripper

R&S Rich and Single Series
Alex Reid
Parker

Saving Forever
Saving Forever - Part 1
Saving Forever - Part 2
Saving Forever - Part 3
Saving Forever - Part 4
Saving Forever - Part 5
Saving Forever - Part 6
Saving Forever Part 7
Saving Forever - Part 8
Saving Forever Boxset Books #1-3

Shifting Desires Series
Jungle Heat

Southern Romance Series
Little Love Affair
Siege of the Heart
Freedom Forever
Soldier's Fortune

Tattooist Series
Confession of a Tattooist
Surrender of a Tattooist
Heart of a Tattooist
Hopes & Dreams of a Tattooist

Tennessee Romance
Whisky Lullaby
Whisky Melody
Whisky Harmony

The Brush Of Love Series
Every Night
Every Day
Every Time
Every Way
Every Touch

The Debt
The Debt: Part 1 - Damn Horse
The Debt: Complete Collection

The University of Gatica Series
The Recruiting Trip

Faster
Higher
Stronger
Dominate
No Rush
University of Gatica - The Complete Series

T.N.T. Series
Troubled Nate Thomas - Part 1
Troubled Nate Thomas - Part 2
Troubled Nate Thomas - Part 3

Undercover Series
Perfect For Me
Perfect For You
Perfect For Us

Unknown Identity Series
Unknown
Unpublished
Unexposed
Unsure
Unwritten
Unknown Identity Box Set: Books #1-3

Unlucky Series

Unlucky in Love
UnWanted
UnLoved Forever

Standalone
Wash
Loving Charity
Summer Lovin'
Love & College
Billionaire Heart
First Love
Frisky and Fun Romance Box Collection
Managing the Bosses Box Set #1-3

Building Billions
Part #3
By Lexy Timms
Copyright 2018

ALL RIGHTS RESERVED. No part of this publication may be reproduced, stored in or introduced into a retrieval system, or transmitted, in any form, or by any means (electronic, mechanical, photocopying, recording, or otherwise) without the prior written permission of both the copyright owner and the above publisher of this book.

This is a work of fiction. Names, characters, places, brands, media, and incidents are either the product of the author's imagination or are used fictitiously. Any resemblance to an actual person, living or dead, events, or locales is entirely coincidental. The author acknowledges the trademarked status and trademark owners of various products referenced in this work of fiction, which have been used without permission. The publication/use of these trademarks is not authorized, associated with, or sponsored by the trademark owners.

All rights reserved.
Building Billions Part #3
Copyright 2018 by Lexy Timms
Cover by: Book Cover by Design[1]

---

1. http://bookcoverbydesign.co.uk/

Building Billions

Part 1
Part 2
Part 3

Find Lexy Timms:

LEXY TIMMS NEWSLETTER:
http://eepurl.com/9i0vD
Lexy Timms Facebook Page:
https://www.facebook.com/SavingForever
Lexy Timms Website:
http://www.lexytimms.com

Want to read more...
For **FREE?**

Sign up for Lexy Timms' newsletter
And she'll send you
A paid read, for FREE!
Sign up for news and updates!
http://eepurl.com/9i0vD

Building Billions Part 3 Blurb

BY USA TODAY BESTSELLING Author, Lexy Timms.

A real man gives up one-night stands for the one he can't stand one night without.

Jimmy didn't believe Ashley when she told him who was behind the fraud within the company. Even when it added up.

He didn't want to believe it because the accused was a father figure to him, the first person to invest in his company and get it started.

Ashley's had no option but to resign from her position. A man who can't trust you is a man you can't keep.

Now Jimmy's on a mission; get Ashley back. She's the best thing that's ever happened to him and he just cannot lose her. He knows he's been an idiot, but is it too late to try and win her back?

They say **LOVE IS A BATTLEFIELD**, not a one-night stand.

Chapter 1

Jimmy

THE COMPANY WAS SAFE, but I felt like shit. As I sipped on my bourbon and stared out the windows of my apartment, my mind rushed back to Ashley. Seeing her empty office down the hallway every morning was too much. Opening my door and hoping she would come walking in like she used to hurt too much. I needed to hire a new accountant for the investors. They had gotten used to that kind of treatment. But no one could provide for them what Ashley had. No one could run the numbers like she could and forecast with the accuracy she was capable of.

The only other person I knew who could do that was already my COO.

My hair was mangled, and my tie was loosened. The buttons on my shirt were broken from tossing and turning the night before. I was sitting in two-day old clothes, staring out a window I had once pressed Ashley up against.

Every part of my apartment was marked with her somehow.

I felt like I was bobbing alone in the sea, lost without an oar or a buoy to mark my way. The city skyline was beginning to tilt as I downed the rest of my drink, and then I let it slip from my fingers.

It clattered to the floor and sprayed the back of my pants.

Every time I closed my eyes, I saw her. Those beautiful eyes and that wondrous smile. I could hear her giggles echoing off the corners of my mind. There were moments throughout the day when I swore I could smell her or hear her padding down the hallway to get coffee after sleeping next to me. Her sleep-tousled hair and her scent lingered in the memories of my senses.

I ached to have her back.

My phone rang out from my room, and I jumped. Was that Ashley? Was she finally calling me back? My socks slipped over the dusty hardwood floor as I ran to my room. I stumbled with my phone in my hands as I took the call, hoping and praying it was her.

Instead, it was the one person I wanted to burn, the one person I wanted to throw screaming and crying off a fucking cliff.

"Jimmy? It's me."

"What the hell do you want, Markus?"

"I want a chance to explain myself," he said.

"Too bad."

"Wait, wait, wait! Jimmy, please."

Maybe it was the desperation in his voice or the defeated sigh that came after. I don't know what possessed me to put the phone back to my ear, but I did. I returned to my chair in silence and flopped down, watching as the sun sank below the skyline of Miami, a city I had quickly come to hate.

"What?" I asked.

"I care about you, Jimmy, and I never meant to hurt you."

"This as good as it gets? Because I've got shit to clean up after what you pulled," I said.

"You're like a son to me, Jimmy. None of this was supposed to come down on your head."

"And what was the grand plan, hm? Keep stealing from underneath my nose? Keep embezzling from a company you helped me create before ratting me out to the media and destroying my reputation? Was that you who started the social media scandal? Because right now, I have a feeling it was."

"No, that wasn't me. You know me better than that."

"No, I sure as hell do not," I said. "You treating me like a son ended when you stole from me. I trusted you. Saw you as a father I never had. Then you went and did exactly what my father did."

"You don't mean that."

"Yes, I do. My father was a drunk and a hack and a fake. Instead of working for his money, he wanted to drink away whatever he could beg from others. That's what you did. You ran your company into the ground, and instead of admitting defeat, you stole from me to fuel a company that should've gone under a long time ago. My father didn't know when to admit he'd failed and start again, and neither do you."

"I was going to pay the money back. I'm serious. Three million dollars, Jimmy."

"Against twenty million!"

"I had it ready. I had a deal sitting on the books that would've recouped the money I took and gotten my company back on the map," he said.

"You wanna know what the shittiest part about all of this is?" I asked.

"What?" he asked.

"Had you come to me with the truth and asked me for money, I would've fucking loaned it to you. In a damn heartbeat."

The silence on the end of the line was deafening. I snickered and shook my head as tears rose to my eyes. I was just drunk enough to allow my emotions to spill over. I was just drunk enough to allow myself to be weak and feel as lost as I felt and to be as angry as I knew I had a right to be.

"I hope you rot," I said.

"Jimmy, wait. Don't hang—"

I hung up the call and immediately dialed Ashley. I knew she would make me feel better. If I could only get her to pick up the phone, it would make everything better. Even if she yelled at me and cussed me out and told me she never wanted to see me again, the simple effort of taking my call would've helped. It would've given me hope.

But like it had been over the last two days, my call went straight to voice mail. I listened to her voice and closed my eyes as her soft tones wafted against my ear. I imagined she was talking to me and smiling with that dazzling smile while her eyes twinkled up at me. She held the stars in her eyes for me, ripped her chest open and handed me her heart. And I had torn her down. Yelled at her. Called her a fucking Nina.

What the hell was I thinking?

I hung up and dialed again, but this time it didn't even ring. It went straight to her voice mail over and over again. She was ignoring me and my calls. There was nothing I could do about that.

There was nothing I could do aside from go to her apartment and sit until she answered.

I threw my phone against the window, and it shattered into a million pieces. I roared into my apartment, my body curling in on itself. I screamed until my face turned red and then screamed until I was hoarse. I put my elbows on my knees and raked my hands through my hair, my voice wheezing through my lips.

I wanted to go to her apartment. I wanted to sit there until she answered. I wanted to linger outside until she was forced to come out and see me, but I wasn't going to harass her. I wasn't going to force her to see me. She was better than that. She deserved better than that.

I loved her more than that.

The phone next to my bed rang out, and I groaned. Who the fuck was trying to call me on a damn Sunday? Didn't people get the picture that I didn't fucking do anything on Sundays? How many times did I have to tell people not to fucking bother me on my motherfucking Sundays?

I stormed into the room and grabbed my phone, ready to slam it against the wall. It kept ringing and ringing in the palm of my hand, waiting for me to answer it.

And when I saw it was Ross, I decided to go ahead and take it.

"What?" I asked.

"The hell's wrong with your cell phone?" he asked.

"It broken," I said flatly.

"Well, let's get you a new one and then get some drinks or something."

"It's Sunday."

"Which means there will be drink specials all day."

"I've got plenty of drinks here," I said.

"Tough. You've wallowed long enough. Let's get you out so you can piece yourself back together for tomorrow."

"I'm not going anywhere today," I said.

"And why not?"

"Because Ashley broke up with me, and I don't feel like going anywhere."

Silence filled the call as I sat on the edge of my bed.

"When did this happen?" Ross asked.

"Wednesday night," I said.

"You've been carrying that around for five days, and you haven't told me about it?"

"Why do you care?" I asked.

"Because I know you love the girl."

"What?"

"Jimmy, I've known you for over twelve damn years. I know you better than anyone else. I know you love Ashley. Why didn't you tell someone?"

"Figured no one cared," I said.

"I care, Jimmy. You've still got me, you know."

"She left, Ross. She broke up with me, and she quit."

"I'm coming to get you. We're going to get you a new phone, we're going to get some drinks, and we're going to talk. And Jimmy?"

"Yeah?"

"Change your clothes. I know you haven't. I can smell you through the damn phone."

I hung up the call and dragged myself to the bathroom. I forced myself to clean up, but I didn't bother trying to shave. I grabbed my keys and my wallet and stuffed everything into pockets. Then I made my way downstairs.

"Get in," Ross said. "Do we need to get you a razor too?"

"Shut up," I said.

We drove to the store, and I picked out whatever newest cell phone Ross had stuck in my hand. I really didn't care. I hooked it up to my cloud account and downloaded everything inside the store, watching as my phone filled up. Applications and documents. Emails and telephone numbers. Text messages and pictures and all sorts of things that reminded me of a life I still had to live.

Fuck. Why did so many people rely on me?

"You ready?" Ross asked.

I was ripped from my trance and found people in the store staring at me.

"Yeah. I'm ready," I said.

"Then let's get some food and some alcohol in you. We need to talk."

"I hate those words," I said.

"Let's get sat down somewhere before we unpack that statement."

Everything was a blur. My phone was ringing out with a notification sound I didn't recognize. I checked every time to see if it was Ashley calling. Emails and text messages and calendar notifications. All bothering me on my one damn day off.

And none of it was what I really wanted anyway.

"So," Ross said. "How did this happen?"

"It all started when a man named Markus came into town."

"Get serious with me. What happened with you and Ashley?" he asked.

"So much shit."

"Then get to talking. I've got all night."

"Things got tense between us with all this ... shit," I said.

"Naturally."

"The stress was affecting her in ways that made me think she was pregnant."

"Like?"

"Pale skin. Mood swings. Not eating. She took that sick day and went to the doctor and got migraine and nausea medication."

"Okay. So what happened?"

"I didn't know why she wasn't telling me she was pregnant, so I took her to lunch. And she didn't eat her lunch. We got it to-go, went to go watch a movie at my place, and I confronted her about it."

"Not good. Because she wasn't pregnant, right?" he asked.

"No, she wasn't, but I was insistent that she was. I got angry that she was lying to me again."

"Hold up, hold up, hold up. Again?"

"She took a couple of sick days when she was still working the balance sheets. One time, she told me her mother wasn't doing well and needed time with her."

"Well, shit. Okay. So you didn't trust her. Was this before or after you told her you trusted her in that investor meeting?" he asked.

"After," I said with a groan.

"That ... was your first fuck up."

"You think I don't know that? Ross, damn it, I thought the woman was pregnant. I was ready to throw down my entire life to make sure she and that child were okay, to make her comfortable and get her to the best doctors and stick by her side through that."

"Yeah, but she wasn't pregnant."

"I get that now," I said. "But that translated into me not believing her when she told me about Markus."

"What?"

"Yeah."

"She knew about Markus?"

"She did," I said.

"When the fuck did this conversation happen? Why the hell am I out of the loop on all of this?"

"It happened Tuesday or Monday. Or sometime at the beginning of the week. I accused her of pinning this on Markus because she was jealous of the time we were spending together."

"No wonder she broke up with you," he said.

"I called her Nina, Ross."

"I'm surprised you're still alive, honestly."

"Thanks."

"No, really. You're shocked she broke up with you?" he asked.

"No, I'm not shocked, but I'm heartbroken. Our company needs her. I need her, Ross."

"Are you wanting to get her back or something?" he asked.

"Yeah. I am."

"I wish I could help, but I have no idea how you're going to pull that off."

"Remind me never to come to you for advice," I said.

"Can we table that for a second and talk about something that's been on my mind?"

"Sure," I said with a sigh. "What's up?"

"I get the inkling we're not the only company Markus stole from."

"What makes you think that?" I asked.

"I did some digging into his company, and they're bad off. Really bad. I mean, thousands of dollars maybe in the bank. He wasn't tanking, Jimmy. He was going bankrupt. Even though he took twenty million dollars from us, it would have easily taken twice that to get him out of hot water."

"Why is this our problem?" I asked.

"I handed over what I found to the police in case they wanted to investigate further, but I can't shake it. And with everything that's happened, I think I should run with it."

"Then you do that. Let me know if I can help you," I said.

"Have you heard from Markus at all?"

"Actually, yeah. He called me from jail this afternoon."

"Is he the reason your phone is broken?"

"He said he still loved me like a son and that he never meant to hurt me."

"Yep. The reason your phone is broken."

"I'm not concerned with him. He's locked up, and with the shit he's done to our company alone, he's going away for a long time," I said.

"So now you're setting your sights on cleaning up the company, right?" Ross asked.

"And getting Ashley back."

"That'll take proving yourself to her. She won't trust you, and if it's really bad, she won't even feel safe around you."

"I know," I said.

"Well, you can't go anywhere but up from here with her. So that's a plus," he said.

"Any idea where I should start? She won't take my phone calls."

"I'm not getting into this lover's quarrel. If you really love her, you're on your own with this one."

"What happened to wanting to be in the loop?" I asked.

"I want to know the drama. I don't want to be a part of it."

"Fine," I said. "To getting Ashley back."

"To getting the company on track," Ross said.

"And fuck everything else."

Then we clinked our glasses, threw back our alcohol, and waited for our food to arrive.

Chapter 2

Ashley

"We should get out and do something," I said.
"Then let's go," Cass said.
"I can't believe that asshole didn't believe me."
"Fuck him. We don't need him."
"But I miss him," I said.
"He was a good one," Cass said.
"I saved him potentially millions. Twice!"
"Hell, yeah, you did!"
"Once with taxes, and once with this fucking Markus shit!"
"You're the boss, girl," she said.
"And Jimmy didn't believe me. Not one fucking word."
"Because he's an asshole."
"But he sent me that email apologizing."
"He did ramble on about it," she said.
"He said he wanted me to come back."
"And we all like it when a tough man begs," she said.
"He sounded like he meant it. I mean, really meant it."
"Yeah, I could see that."
"He also said he would talk anywhere I wanted. So I'm in control now."
"And we like control. Powerful women take control," she said.
"I saved his company. Not him. I'm the one who saw it. Not him."
"Because he's an asshole who doesn't deserve his company," she said.
"He'll fail without me," I said.
I stopped pacing around my apartment as I leaned against the wall.
"The investors will be lost without me," I said.
"Can I stop being your hype girl and talk to you for a second?"

"What's up?" I asked.

"I think you're crazy for quitting your job."

"I couldn't stay, Cass. You know I can't separate my emotions from my situations very well."

"Ashley, you're the strongest woman I know. You take care of your mother, and you've paved your own pathway toward an awesome career. You're intelligent, and you rock it like a fucking rock star. You're incredible in more ways than one, but everyone has room to grow. Everyone has things they can work on."

"He called me a 'Nina,' Cass."

"And that was a bullshit move on his part," she said. "But you shouldn't have quit. You built a life on that salary, and all of this is going to affect your credit. You won't be able to afford this apartment. You won't be able to pay your mother's medical bills. You won't be able to afford taking care of Chipper. You did this with your emotions, and you've put yourself in a rough position."

"You ready to hear the adult side of me talk now?" I asked.

"Sure," she said.

"Did you really think I was going to be spending all that money on my paychecks in one get-go? Between the savings account I already had and the money I threw in there because it never got spent, I've got enough to get me through the year-long lease on this apartment."

"No shit. Seriously?" she asked.

"I've also got one more full paycheck coming my way and a small minor one. And there's my severance package."

"You really thought that out, didn't you?"

"I did. Cass, that man debased me in the middle of his office. For the first time since I'd known Jimmy, I was scared around him. He scared me with that look in his eye, with the protective anger he threw my way when I accused Markus. That was protective anger he should've had for me, but he didn't."

"You know that man cares about you," she said.

"If you were in my shoes, what would you have done? Because I know you, Cass. I know you would've left his ass crying in the damn rain."

"And I'm currently single, if you haven't noticed. It's not fun in Miami like you think it is. Guys like a nice time, but no one wants to settle down."

"Are you saying you want to settle down?"

"Hell, no. I'm saying you're the kind of woman who does. I know you want a family. I know you want to paint that life for yourself, but the men in Miami don't want that."

"And you think Jimmy does?"

"I think he was getting there. You said he fought you on being pregnant. Did you ever stop to think that he was that way because he was ready to provide for you because of it?"

My mind rushed back to that argument as tears rose to my eyes. Cass was right. That had been why Jimmy was fighting me on it.

"Shit," I said.

"I'm not saying to give the man a second chance, because I'm not sure he deserves it. I am saying to remove your anger from the situation and try to look at what happened from a logical perspective."

"Did you ever think you'd be saying those words to me?" I asked.

"Never in a million fucking years. Now, can we get the hell out of this apartment? Chipper's asleep, and I'm starving."

"Lunch sounds awesome."

"And it's on me, Miss Jobless."

I made sure Chipper had water and some food before I grabbed my things. We walked down to Cass's car and got in so we could head to lunch. I looked down into my purse and saw my phone rattling around like the brick it was. I hadn't had it on in days. I'd turned it off Thursday night, and I hadn't turned it back on since. I didn't want to. I didn't want to see all the missed calls and messages I probably had from Jimmy. If the email he sent me was a look into his mindset, then he was probably trying to get me to pick up, calling over and over, trying to get me to talk with him.

"Thanks for banging down my door this morning," I said.

"You turned your phone off. I didn't have a choice," Cass said.

"Do you think I should turn it back on?"

"Do you want to be bombarded with the messages you know you'll have from the asshat?"

"That what we're calling him now? The asshat?"

"Until he redeems himself or falls off the face of the earth, yes," she said.

"I feel miserable," I said.

"I know you do. I can't imagine what you're going through right now, but I'm here for you. You know that, right?"

"Yeah, I know you are. It's just hard, knowing I'll have to apply for jobs and do all sorts of interviews while my heart is breaking," I said.

"Can you claim 'Saving Big Steps' on your resume?"

I giggled and shook my head as we pulled into my favorite lunch spot.

"Oh, hibachi. I love these places. There's always so much food to take home."

"And that's why we're here. Lunch and dinner," Cass said.

"Does that mean you're staying for dinner?" I asked.

"Honey, I'm staying through dinner. You're not getting rid of me until you turn that phone back on."

"You have to work tomorrow."

"Which is why you're going to turn your phone on tomorrow," she said.

"What about all the messages and missed phone calls?"

"Honestly? You're going to have to talk with him at some point in time. Even if you take the severance package and leave, you can't shut him out like that. Believe me, I've tried. Men are persistent when the pussy's good."

"Seriously?" I asked.

"You had a billionaire wrapped around your finger. That's all the proof I need about yours."

"You're insane," I said.

"And you do need to talk to him eventually. You can't avoid him forever."

"Why not?" I asked.

"Because that isn't what strong, independent women do, Ashley."

"I hate being an adult."

"We all do," she said. "Now come on, let's go get us some seats."

Cass dragged me into the restaurant, and we sat down with a family. A man, a woman, and their four kids. The woman looked frazzled and had bags underneath her eyes. The children were rambunctious at best, and she was constantly having to tell them to sit down or sit still or stop what they were doing.

And her husband was looking at her as if she was the center of his universe.

"You owe him a conversation," Cass said.

"Who?" I asked.

"Jimmy."

"How does any of this translate into owing him anything?" I asked.

"You having your phone off means he's probably worrying about you, and you're intentionally doing that to him. Even if the conversation is short and you tell him you aren't coming back, you owe it to him to talk to him."

"I already did. When I broke up with him."

"And now he's realized he was wrong. He watched a man he cared about greatly get arrested in the middle of a damn investor's meeting."

"How do you know that?" I asked.

"It's been all over the news for days. Have you not turned on anything?"

"No, I haven't."

"You need to talk to him. You owe him that after quitting through an email. You could break up with him face-to-face, but you couldn't quit your job face-to-face?"

"Why do you always have to be right?" I said.

"It's a curse, I know. We'll enjoy this food and enjoy it again tonight, but when we wake up in the morning, that phone goes on and you pull your big girl panties up."

"Fine," I said. "Can we get drinks too?"

"Honey, when has that ever been a question with me?"

Chapter 3

Jimmy

"I fucking knew it," Ross said. "Look at this."

It boiled my blood to see the initials 'LR' on that sheet of fucking paper.

"What company is this?" I asked.

"Ace-Landic. They're an energy company based out of Miami."

"The bright blue building on the other side of town?"

"That one. I have a feeling if I keep digging, it's not going to get any better," he said.

Ross was sitting at my desk as we combed through the files of other companies around us. Markus had deep roots in this area, and we were beginning to figure out why. One of the detectives from the agency we hired came back interested in exploring Ross's theory further. So he tapped into his resources and got us some company files we were going over. I didn't ask the man who he got them from, and I didn't care. If Markus was stealing from these companies, they needed to know.

And he needed to go down for it.

"Those initials are scattered throughout Ace-Landic's files," Ross said.

"I see them scattered through Harold & Lace. It's not much, but it's there. He's in them too."

"Harold & Lace? The sex shop?" he asked.

"Yeah. Apparently, Markus didn't fucking care who he stole from," I said.

"How was he sinking his claws into these people? Was he chummy with everyone?" he asked.

"I don't know. All I'm doing is highlighting the initials and handing everything back over to the PI. He can be our go-to between the police and this investigation."

I had no doubt in my mind Ashley had been right. Even if there was the smallest shred of evidence that meant Markus could've been innocent, the flood of paperwork in front of me with those initials overruled it. That man had his hands in so many pies, it boggled my mind. That was how he was finding the separate funds to keep his company afloat.

He was embezzling from everyone around him.

"Why doesn't he let his company sink? Cut the loss and try again? I don't get it," I said.

"Pride," Ross said. "It's the downfall of every man."

"Don't I fucking know it," I said.

"I think there's still a chance you could get her back, you know."

"I'm not so sure about that," I said.

"I think you won't know until you try, and Ashley is worth more than a try or two."

"She won't even take my calls. How the hell am I supposed to—?"

My office phone rang, and I rolled my eyes. Life never stopped for one of the top businesses in the world. It was probably my PR department wanting to track me down for an official quote. I still wasn't ready to give it, and I wouldn't until I knew what I wanted to say.

"Jimmy?"

My body froze in my seat when I heard her voice.

"Ashley," I said. "Good morning."

Ross's eyes widened as he began to gather everything off my desk.

"I wanted to let you know I'm coming by the office this morning. You know, to pick up things from my desk."

"Okay. That's fine. Do you want me to unlock your office for you?" I asked.

"I've got my keys. It's not a big deal. I wanted to let you know in case ..."

I closed my eyes and allowed her voice to take me over. Ross patted me on the shoulder before he left, taking all the paperwork with him. I reclined back in my chair, listening to her soft breathing come through the phone.

"No one's taking that office from you," I said. "You come by whenever you want."

"Okay," Ashley said.

The call hung up, and I couldn't focus. Every time a person passed by, I whipped my head up. I heard the elevator doors open, and hope flooded my veins. I listened to the familiar patter of footsteps as she came down the hallway.

Ashley.

My Ashley.

She was a fucking sight for sore eyes.

I watched her walk to her office, and I took her all in, the way her clothes draped around her body and the way she stood tall and proud. She knew her worth now. She walked with confidence, and it pulled a smile across my face. I felt hope seeing her, even though I was watching her pack up her things. I stood up from my desk and smoothed my suit jacket down, trying to calm my nerves.

I had to stay calm.

If I was going to get her to talk to me, I had to stay calm.

"Ashley, could we talk for a second?"

I watched her eyes flutter up to mine as she looked at me from beneath her lashes. She could still mesmerize me with her stare. Her body still called to me. I cried out for her to smile, to grace me with the comfort her twinkling eyes brought.

Instead, I saw hesitance tinged with a bit of fear.

"Please," I said.

"I mean, I guess. I don't really have a lot of time, though," Ashley said.

"That's fine. I'll take whatever time you can give me," I said.

I pulled her into my office and shut the door behind her. She set her box down on the floor at her feet, her eyes looking around my office. She was avoiding me, avoiding my gaze. I had hurt this woman beyond all personal comprehension, and I had no idea where to begin.

"I know you're probably in here because you didn't want to cause a scene," I said.

Ashley sighed and shook her head.

"Please, don't go," I said. "Please, give this company another chance."

"You don't want me to give you another chance?" she asked.

"Would you give me another chance? Because if you're willing to do it, then I'm willing to do whatever it takes to get you back," I said.

"And why should I do that?" she asked.

"I believe you. About everything. Ashley, he's done this to so many other companies. Ross and I were going through paperwork and—"

"Should you be talking about this with someone who doesn't work for you?" she asked.

"Please. You were right. About everything. I believe you. Everything you said. All of it was right."

She scoffed as a tainted smile crossed her face.

"You should've believed me before."

"I know. I'm sorry, Ashley. Please, tell me what I can do. This company needs you. I—"

Her eyes panned over to me as the words caught in my throat. The pain, it was unbearable. The pain swirling behind her eyes made me sick. How could I have done this to her? How could I have said all those things? How could I have lost my temper and taken Markus's side and left her out in the cold like I had?

Why the fuck did I let her walk away at that damn bar?

"I'm sorry," I said.

"You can't even say it."

"Let me take you out."

"What?" Ashley asked.

"Let me take you out. To dinner, or drinks. Hell, I'll take you to Italy for pastries. But let me take you out so we can talk longer. So we can talk about this."

"No," she said plainly.

"Rome."

"No."

"Paris."

"No."

"The Maldives. Bora Bora. Antarctica."

"Why would I want to go to Antarctica?" she asked.

"The Northern Lights. I hear they're beautiful year-round up there," I said.

"No," she said breathlessly.

She bent down to pick up her things, but I stopped her. The least I could do was help her carry everything out. I picked up her box and followed her out of my office, putting on my strongest demeanor. Ashley was ignoring me, not looking back to see if I was even following her. I kept my eyes ahead of me and nodded at people as we walked by. I put on the face of a man who was in control, but inside, I was dying.

Decaying.

Crumbling without Ashley.

This company needed her. I needed her. Why the hell couldn't I say that to her? We were going to drown without her. The books she looked after and the notes she kept, they were in a language none of us could understand. Calculations that had been bypassed and passwords that had been set. PDF documents that were half-done and projections even Ross couldn't figure out how she'd gotten.

We needed her.

I walked all the way to her car, and she popped her trunk. I settled everything down, and she shut it with a slam, not waiting for me to get my fingers out of the way. I ripped my hands back barely in time, watching as the car rocked on its chassis.

"If you don't want to stay, then at least explain the company books you kept to someone," I said.

"Jimmy."

"No one understands them. Ross hardly does," I said.

"I highly doubt that."

"You really don't get how invaluable you are to us, or any company that will hire you. Your mind is incredible, Ashley. The wealth of knowledge and the way you compute information at lightning speed, it's unprecedented," I said.

I saw a spark in her eye, and it ignited a fire in the pit of my stomach.

"You don't have to explain them to me, but explain them to someone. Go over them with Ross. Show him your calculations and equations. Walk him through it. We'll be lost for months without you, trying to decipher your tallies and your PDFs."

"You're giving me too much credit," she said.

"If anything, I haven't given you enough. Ever."

Her eyes turned up to me, and I could've sworn I saw them twinkling with the shadow of a smile.

"I'll beef up your severance package," I said. "I'll give you more than HR will ever offer you. Just explain them to someone. That's all I'm asking."

"I'll think about it," she said.

"That's all I'm asking."

She allowed me to open her door for her as she stepped into her car. I backed up as she cranked it up, knowing full good and well she'd run me over if she got the chance. I watched her back out of the parking space and meander through the parking garage, the car creating distance between us.

But as I watched her face in the side mirror of her car, I saw her eyes glance back at me before she disappeared around the corner.

And it filled me with a hope that almost hurt to contain.

Chapter 4

Ashley

I sat on the porch of my apartment staring out over the city of Miami. I couldn't get my interaction with Jimmy yesterday out of my head. All he wanted was to sit down and talk, take me somewhere and talk things out to see where we could go from there. I couldn't help feeling I had been a bit cruel to him by refusing him something he so desperate to have. I replayed the moment over and over again in my head as the bustling city I had come to love came alive with the sun hanging in the sky.

But I felt like giving him that conversation was validating that it was okay for him to do what he'd done to me. For him to constantly question what I was saying about my own body. I had to slap him with a bag full of pregnancy tests to prove I wasn't pregnant. He was hell-bent on the fact that he was right about something happening to my body. And what was worse was that he felt I wouldn't have come to him with something like that. He'd believed it was in my personality somewhere to keep something so intimate and so important from him

Like I hadn't come to care about him at all.

He hurt me, and I was tired of it. Over and over during the past week, he had done nothing but hurt me. He'd pushed me away and acted like I didn't exist rather than have an adult conversation when I wanted to have one with him. Now I was supposed to bend to his will? After him asking once after finding out I was, in fact, right about Markus? Why couldn't he have believed me in the first place? It wasn't like I was concocting stories and trying to tie a knot with only one loose end. Everything I was talking about made sense.

Why did it take talking to someone else to figure out what I was telling him was right?

I couldn't understand it, and thinking about it made me angry all over again. Was I only some stupid woman who ran numbers and looked pretty at his side? Did my opinion not have any validation? First, it was my insistence on Nina becoming an issue. He didn't listen, and she became an issue. Then, it was Markus and my insistence that he was behind all of this, and what was Jimmy's reaction? Not to brush me off like some over-concerned kept woman of his, but to call me the one name that disgusted him more than his father's.

That was his response to my findings.

I wiped at the tears threatening to fall down my face. I was a strong woman, an independent woman. I wasn't going to allow a man like Jimmy to tear me down any longer. I hadn't heard from him since I cleaned out my office yesterday, which meant he had given up on me.

And maybe it was for the best.

Maybe we were simply toxic for one another.

My next step was to find a job. Since I wasn't going back to Big Steps, I needed to find another job to help me with bills. With my mother's bills. With my mother's nursing home fees. I had my savings set aside, but those would only cover my car insurance and my rent. I would need money within the next month to keep up with things like electricity and water and my mother's nursing home account.

Otherwise, I would have to start picking and choosing what I paid.

I stood up from my chair and grabbed my purse. I looked over at my personal laptop and shoved it into the crook of my arm. If I was going to find a job, then I needed to start putting in my resume. I spent all of last night updating it to reflect my prior job history and all of the things I had done, and it was time to start putting it in at various places in Miami.

I would even look outside of Miami if I had to.

I left my apartment and started walking down the block. There was a coffeehouse I had come to enjoy, and I didn't have to use up gas in my car to get there. I would have to pull myself up by my bootstraps and start pinching pennies again. That meant eating all the food I had here before going to the grocery store and giving myself over to noodles and sauce again. I sighed as I walked into the coffee shop and dug around for a few dollars. It made me sick to break a hundred-dollar bill for a cup of coffee, so I scrounged around for change to use.

I took my empty cup and filled it with a strong brew. The scent was heavenly, and a hefty dose of sweet cream would make it perfect. I took my coffee, sat in a corner, and then used their internet to start my own job hunt.

I clicked through accountant positions and applied to each one that had a salary over sixty thousand a year. I would have to downgrade back to my original living standards on something like that, but it would be doable. I could ride out my current lease on my savings, move without incurring penalties, and slip back into my old life.

My old world before Jimmy happened.

A sadness sank to the bottom of my gut. As I dumped my application into multiple job opening descriptions, my body felt like it was growing heavier. Life had seemed so easy and simple when I was working for Jimmy. Even before things had kicked off between us, I had enjoyed it. I smiled getting up for work, and I took care of my appearance because I wanted to. I felt like I was doing the world a bit of good by being the investor's accountant.

I was treated with respect and regarded as not only a corporate employee but as a friend. I was going to miss Ross and those investors. Even Mr. Matthews and his checks that never cleared.

I hated to admit it, but a part of me was going to miss Jimmy. I was going to miss seeing his face and listening to his laughter and sitting in front of him while he smiled at me.

Had I made a mistake in quitting?

No, I hadn't. Things could never go back to the way they were. I would always feel weird around Jimmy, and people would wonder if I was screwing around with corporate to get to where I was. I would look around my office and see Jimmy in all of it, and it would do nothing to help my broken heart. I would never be able to heal if I had stayed. I would've never been able to shake the care and compassion that had grown between Jimmy and me.

It would kill me to look out into the hallway and see his office, knowing I couldn't go to him.

I put my resume in for seventeen job openings before an email dropped into my inbox. I clicked over to it and read the title as the blood drained from my face. The nursing home was incurring another monthly fee hike of fifty more dollars.

Had I still been working at Big Steps, that wouldn't have been an issue. Now that I was jobless, that was a massive issue. I flipped back over and applied to seven more jobs as my palms began to sweat.

How was I going to afford fifty more dollars a month?

I wanted my mother to be in the best care Miami had to offer, even if she didn't understand that was what she had. She was comfortable with that place, and the staff knew her well. I wasn't going to move her to try and help with my bills. I would cut back on my own spending and live out of my car if that was necessary.

Wait, could I really do something like that?

I shook the thought from my head as I sipped my coffee. I closed my laptop and sat there as my mother poured into my mind. That would be a good thing to go do today. I could go visit my mother and see how she was doing. Seeing her always made me feel better, even if it was only temporary. If she was lucid, she might have advice for me in the position I was in.

But if she wasn't ...

I drew in a deep breath and gathered my things. I was going to go see my mother. I was a daughter on the verge of a nervous breakdown, and I needed to see my mother.

So that was where I headed.

I pulled into the nursing home and walked through the double doors. The women at the desk greeted me with a smile as I turned the corner. That was good. Grim looks usually meant my mother was having a rough day. I walked all the way down the hall, turned into her room, and I found her staring out the window, sitting upright with her eyes focused and her beautiful white hair done up with her bobby pins.

She had taken the time to put herself together this morning.

That meant she was doing really well.

"Hey, Mom."

"Is that my daughter I hear?" she asked.

She turned and smiled at me, and I ran into her arms.

"Oh, dear. Sweetheart. Oh, what's wrong?" my mother asked.

"I'm so glad you're having a good day," I said.

"I know you, Ashley. I know when something's wrong. Talk to me about it. Like you used to?"

"Do you remember meeting Jimmy?" I asked.

"Who's Jimmy?"

"Tall man. Dark hair. Talked with you about our wedding."

"Wedding? You got married?" she asked.

"No, no. I ... look, never mind. How are you doing, Mom? How did you sleep last night?"

"Terribly. The thunderstorms were awful."

"They did rock the house a bit," I said with a grin.

"The lightning is always beautiful, but I really could do without that thunder."

"You know thunder is a byproduct of the heat from the lightning piercing the air. When the air comes back together, it makes a clapping sound that we interpret as thunder."

"How did you get to be so smart?"

"I get it from my momma," I said with a smile.

"You sure didn't get it from your father. That man was an idiot."

I laughed as I scooted up a chair next to my mother's bed.

"Got any big plans for your day?" I asked.

"Nope. Just resting for the day. I didn't get much sleep with all the thunder, so I'm taking it easy."

"Got any handsome visitors coming later on? You sure do look spiffy," I said.

"Why do I have to get dressed up for a man? What if I want to look good for myself?"

"I see where I got my independence from."

"Again, you didn't get it from your father. That man was as emotionally clingy as they came."

"The more you talk about him, the more I wonder why you married him," I said with a giggle.

"Beats me," she said with a shrug. "I plead temporary insanity."

The two of a shared a laugh, and it lifted my spirits. These moments were becoming fewer and farther between. I felt like a regular mother and daughter, bonding over our own emotions and senses of humor. This was what our relationship would've been like had it not been for this damned disease. I would have these moments with her every day. In my own apartment. I'd move her in with me, and we would watch the sun go down below the city every night with a sharp glass of wine.

That was what my life was supposed to look like. Not moping around brokenhearted and jobless.

I sighed as I watched my mother's eyes lost focus. It was coming. The storms that had raged last night were beginning to cloud my mother's memory. She whipped her head around, her eyes darting around the room.

And that quickly, her lucidity was gone.

"Hello?" my mother asked.

"Yes, ma'am?"

"Who are you?" she asked.

"I'm a friend of your daughter's. She wanted me to come check on you," I said.

"Well, tell her she needs to come see me. I haven't seen that child in weeks. What kind of girl stuffs her mother away in a place like this and never comes to visit?"

I felt my heart drop to my toes. Her Alzheimer's was getting so bad, she thought I was abandoning her, not remembering our visits for weeks at a time.

I wanted to puke.

"She comes by a lot," I said. "A few times a week."

"Well, she isn't here now. Some girl she turned out to be. Takes after her father, you know. Flakey and flimsy and not a decent bone in her body."

"I'm sure you don't mean that," I said.

"I do!" she said. "Why hasn't she come to visit me?"

"She has," I said breathlessly.

"Why are you crying? You don't have a reason to cry."

"It's been a rough week or so," I said.

"That my daughter's excuse too?" she asked.

I couldn't take it anymore. I was strong but not this strong. She was looking right at me and spewing vile where only seconds ago, there was love. I got up from my seat and leaned into her, pressing a kiss to her forehead.

But she ripped away and began slamming her hand on the red button at her bedside.

"Who are you? Why are you touching me? Nurse? Nurse!"

I sighed and shook my head as I turned away from her. The nurse from the station at the corner came running in and gave me a sympathetic look. She went over and sat on the side of my mom's bed to try to calm her down, and I couldn't stay for it this time. I knew what would happen. My mother would get combative and call out for me, demand someone call me even though I was looking right at her. She would spit or kick or possibly slap one of the nurses. Then they would have to control her with medication while she yelled out to not stick her with "that thing."

It was all becoming too much.

I walked down the hallway, leaving the pieces of my shattered heart behind. I felt empty. Lost. Alone in the abyss of my life. My mother was knocking on death's door with every passing day, and it was becoming more expensive to keep up with what she needed. She would need an adjustment to her medication soon enough, and that would cost more out of my pocket. If she took another spill and hurt herself, that would mean more hospital visits.

Which meant more hospital bills. Which meant more money.

It was all overwhelming, and a part of me wished I could call Jimmy and talk with him about it.

As I sat in my car looking out over the nursing home, I had to urge to drive and see him. It would be easy to head to Jimmy's, a straight shot down the main road and two left-hand turns. He was maybe six minutes away. Six minutes sat between me and his comforting embrace. Me and his chest that would soak up my tears. Me and those lips he would press into the top of my head.

I shook the thought away and fought it with all my might. I pulled out of the parking space and forced myself to go home, back to the apartment I could no longer afford without wiping my savings account clean.

Then, I thought back to Jimmy's words and what he had said about my severance package.

If I explained the books to someone, that would get me more money. That money would go a long way in helping with Mom and her bills. Depending on how much it was, it might even get me through the year with her bills, which would be outstanding. It meant I would have a little more financial freedom and breathing room to find a job.

All I would have to do would be to explain my notations to someone.

It didn't even have to be to Jimmy. It could be to Ross, and he would be the better person to explain it to, anyway. He was the numbers guy. He would latch on quicker than Jimmy would, and I would be able to trust him to take care of what I'd done, keeping the organization I had laid in place and sticking with the projection equations I had altered to predict with greater accuracy for the investors.

I didn't trust Jimmy to pay attention if I was in the room talking to him.

I parked my car and hoisted my laptop into the crook of my arm. I walked to the elevator, my mind in a haze. In a span of four days, my life had completely fallen apart. The dream job I'd acquired was tainted by a relationship that had gone sour. A man I had come to care for and trust had become a phantom memory of my father, the anger I'd seen in his eyes every day growing up and the yelling that always took place between my mother and him.

I'd seen my father in Jimmy's eyes that day, and it ruined everything for me.

I stood in the elevator and closed my eyes. I allowed it to take me on a little trip before I pressed the button for the fourteenth level. I forced my mind to stop, shut down everything, reboot, and cast aside all the issues that no longer deserved my attention.

I walked into my apartment and dropped everything onto the couch. I grabbed my glass of stale wine and went to sit out on the porch. It was my favorite place to be, smelling the salt air and feeling the wind whipping around my body. I would miss this view. Even after seeing it every day for an entire year to come, I knew I would miss it once I moved.

It would be hard to go back to the brick wall views I'd been accustomed to before my life had changed, before I'd been promoted and knew what it felt like to be able to take care of myself for once.

I drank back the last of the wine before I set my glass between my legs. I slumped into my chair and closed my eyes as I listened to the city hustle below me. Maybe things would turn out okay. Maybe one of the corporate positions I had applied to would consider me qualified enough for the position. Maybe one of the starter businesses who needed a lone accountant could hire me for the money they were saying they could, and everything would work itself out.

Or maybe it wouldn't.

And that little doubtful sliver of me yelled the loudest in the recesses of my mind.

Maybe, just maybe, things wouldn't be okay.

Chapter 5

Jimmy

I was sitting across the table with Ross as I held my drink in my hand. I needed to get out and get my mind off the shitty week I'd endured. I still had one day to go, but I knew I wouldn't make it until Friday night.

I needed a break from all the shit we'd figured out.

"I handed over everything to the PI this morning," Ross said.

"I can't believe he fucking robbed all of my damn companies," I said. "I'll never see that money again."

"Thankfully, not all of our subcompanies were hit. Just the two. I still couldn't figure out how those other two random companies in Miami lined up with Markus, though."

"Ashley would've been able to find it," I said.

"Have you heard from her at all?" he asked.

"Not a damn peep."

"Do you think she'll take the offer for the beefy severance package?"

"I'm hoping so because I don't understand a damn word in her files," I said.

"I understand some of it, but it'll still take me some time to decipher what was going on in her head with those equations. There are multiple steps missing, all of which I assume she did in her head."

"Is it bad I still want to show her all of this? All of this stuff we've found on Markus?"

"No, but you shouldn't. She doesn't work with the company anymore, and that's privileged information."

"It might help get her back. If she knows we're running with this because of what she found," I said.

"You can't give her specifics, and you sure as hell can't show her the paperwork."

"I miss her, Ross."

"I know. The company misses her. With her eyes and the way she could speed-read, we could've had this shit turned over and wrapped up days ago," he said.

"She's a valuable asset."

"The best," he said.

"We have to get her back."

"I know we do, but setting personal feelings aside in favor of professional ones is hard. And you can't blame Ashley for that."

"I don't blame her. For anything," I said.

"Have you told her that?"

"She hasn't called me," I said.

"Why the hell are you waiting for her to call you?"

"Because she didn't take my calls for two damn days, Ross."

"Doesn't mean you stop trying," he said.

"Why would I keep doing something over and over again if it doesn't get me the results I want?"

"Because you're not building a business, you're chasing a woman," he said.

"I could ring that man's fucking neck," I said.

"That's probably how Ashley feels about you, to be honest."

"Why did I not believe her?"

"Because you were blinded by your love and trust in Markus. It would be like accusing Ashley's mother of embezzling from the company. Ashley probably would've had the same reaction. What was unnecessary was all the shit you said to her after you didn't believe her."

"Well, my not believing her didn't help," I said.

"What you really should've done was gone after her when she left the bar."

"I keep replaying that night over and over in my head. I was so angry at her. You know I asked her if she was going to apologize for accusing Markus? I was still on fucking Markus!"

"I'm not saying you're not climbing Everest here, but I'm saying there are some men that have come back from worse. It takes time, perseverance, and a delicate dance between being annoying and giving her space," he said.

"You know I couldn't tell her the other day that I needed her?"

"What?" he asked.

"Yeah. She was standing right there in my office, and I told her the damn company needed her."

"Well, we do."

"Yeah. Then I went to go say it and stopped! Like I hadn't learned my fucking lesson."

"Why did you stop?" he asked.

"I don't know, Ross."

"You do. You're a grown ass man who can filter through his emotions. Why didn't you tell her?"

"Because."

I threw the rest of my drink back and set it on a passing tray.

"Because I was scared I would tell her, and it wouldn't make a damn bit of difference."

"There it is. Now, I'm telling you this with all the respect in my soul, Jimmy. You don't have home-court advantage here. You aren't the one who gets to keep your emotions close to your chest. You're the one bleeding in the street still crawling toward her apartment. That's you."

"I know. I'm so damn angry. I've never been this angry. Not at my father. Not at my life. Not at my idiotic professors in college. Never. I have no idea what to do with all this anger, Ross."

"I can't help you there," he said. "But bourbon always helps me."

"She doesn't want anything to do with me."

"If you keep that train of thought rattling around in your mind, then you'll convince yourself of it," he said.

"I have to find a way to put the company's needs above my own right now," I said.

"Well, that took a turn. Why?" he asked.

"Because this thing with Markus goes deep. There are two companies completely unrelated to us that have no idea what's been done to them. I'm hoping the PI will reach out to them. Now that we have proof of all this, we have to keep digging. We have to figure out how deep this goes with this greedy asshole."

"If that's the personal venture you want to take on, then fine. The police have already booked and charged him, so I'm not sure if we'll be able to tack this stuff onto his charges already," he said.

"I'll figure it out. But now that Markus is out of the picture, two things have to happen. We need to find a new investor, and we need to right our ship. None of the investors bailed, but they're wary of investing. Until we can provide them clear and concise balance sheets due to Markus being incarcerated, I don't think we'll see a cent from them."

"Then that's what we'll focus on," Ross said.

My phone rang in my pocket, and I jumped. Every time it rang, I thought it was Ashley. At the very least, I hoped it was Ashley. But my vision dripped with red when I saw what number was calling.

I didn't want to talk to that asshole.

I ignored the call and stuffed it back into my pocket. I felt my anger subsiding as another drink was set in front of me, but part of me did feel bad. I was denying Markus the one thing Ashley was denying me. A chance to talk. But he'd betrayed me in all the worst ways possible. He'd taken my love for him and twisted it to his own selfish whims.

Holy shit, was that what Ashley thought I'd done?

"Who was that?" Ross asked.

"Jail," I said.

"That man's still calling you?" he asked.

"Do you think I should've answered it?"

"Hell, no. You owe him nothing."

"Like Ashley owes me nothing?"

"Look, this is different. That man stole millions from you. You said some shit that hurt Ashley, but you didn't betray her trust, years of trust after cultivating a familial relationship with her. Don't do that to yourself."

"I denied him the one thing Ashley's denying me. I kind of know how he feels, wanting to talk to the person he wronged," I said.

"Jimmy, I hate it when you draw these kinds of conclusions."

"Because you know you don't have a leg to stand on in the argument," I said. "That man was like a father to me, the only real father figure I ever had."

"I don't know what to tell you. All I could see was the anger in your eyes when you looked down at your phone. With how angry you still are, you'll accomplish nothing talking to him in this state of mind," he said.

"Now that makes sense," I said.

"To things that make sense," Ross said.

"To things that finally fall back together," I said.

We clinked our glasses and sat in silence as my mind started to swirl. I still cared about Markus. I still wanted him to be okay. Through all the shit he put me through and stole from my company, I couldn't shake the years we'd had together. Without his advice, I would've never climbed to the top. Yes, he stole from me, but I succeeded beyond my wildest dreams because of him. He made me into the businessman I was today, and with the charges being brought against him, he would lose everything before he left prison.

Would it make any difference if I kept investigating him?

If I drove a man into the ground who was already bleeding out, would it make me feel any better about what happened?

Chapter 6

Ashley
Friday

I was having no luck in the job department. Every time I turned around, an email with the word "rejection" was being sent to me. All the corporate jobs that would allow me to keep up the life I was living said I didn't have enough work experience or that my experience was too tailored for them, and the jobs that wanted me to interview couldn't pay me the bottom-basement of what I needed to live in Miami, much less keep my mother where she was.

The only other avenue I had was Jimmy's offer. I didn't have any other choice. With interviews on the books for jobs that paid close to nothing for my expertise, I would need that severance package. It wouldn't carry me far. If I was lucky, it would get me to the end of the year, but it would give me enough time to figure out what I was going to do about a job.

I picked up my phone and called Jimmy's office as I sat on my porch.

"Jimmy Sheldon."

"Hey, Jimmy."

"Ashley? Is that you?" he asked.

"Yeah."

"Hello. Sorry. I'm ... a bit shocked to hear from you," he said.

"Don't worry. It's understandable. Don't take it for more than what it is, though."

"I wouldn't dream of it. What do you need?" he asked.

"What makes you think I need something?"

"Because I'm not reading into more than it is."

"Fair enough. I wanted to talk with you more about that severance package and scheduling a time to sit down with Ross and talk him through everything," I said.

"Perfect. I was hoping you would take me up on that. Even with Ross unpacking what he already has now, it's taken us days to get through four documents."

"Interesting. That's fine. When do you want me to meet with him?"

"We're busy all day today, but I do have something important I wish to discuss with you," he said.

"What about?" I asked.

"Would it be possible for you to meet me at my apartment this evening?"

"No."

"I would bring you into my office, but this isn't something I want others to overhear. It's a personal project Ross and I have taken on, and I'd like your input. As a consultant. I'd be willing to pay you for your time."

Well, going over to his house wasn't him taking me out to dinner, and if he was offering more money, I could sure as hell use it.

"Okay," I said with a sigh. "What time?"

"Seven sound good to you?" Jimmy asked.

"Sure. I'll see you then."

"I'll leave the door unlocked."

I rolled my eyes as I hung up the phone. I couldn't shake the idea that he was trying to get me alone, but part of me was excited to go over and see him. I walked inside, shut the door behind me, and then proceeded to piece myself together. I left plenty of food and water for Chipper in my room, so he could curl up on my bed with his toys. Then I headed for my car.

It took effort not to speed all the way to Jimmy's place.

The moment the elevator doors opened, I groaned. Jimmy was cooking. Why the hell was he cooking? I walked to his front door and opened it up as the smell of homemade lasagna hit my nostrils.

What was the man thinking? Why was he cooking for me?

I loved his cooking.

He knew I loved his cooking.

"Hope you don't mind," Jimmy said. "I got hungry and figured you might be too."

"I'm sticking with water tonight," I said.

"Lemonade okay?" he asked.

"You made lemonade?"

"I did."

"Sure. Lemonade's fine, then."

I walked back into his kitchen and found his table set for two. I shrugged my coat off and threw it over the chair before sitting down on my side of the table.

My side.

The side I'd always taken up during our morning coffee ventures.

"Do you want a salad or garlic bread?" Jimmy asked.

"Why can't I have both?" I asked.

He set the food down on the table, but I only picked at my salad. The food smelled delicious, but I wasn't in the mood to eat it. I could feel Jimmy's eyes on me as he ate his food, the silence between us at an uncomfortable high.

"What do you need me to consult on?" I asked.

"First off, I need you to hear me when I tell you I believe you about Markus."

"I know," I said.

"I'm sorry for everything I said to you. It was uncalled for, and no amount of stress should've ever led me to say those things to you, Ashley."

"I know," I said.

"I'm investigating Markus myself. Well, Ross and me and a PI."

"What?"

"Yeah. When Markus was hauled out in handcuffs, Ross's primary concern was that Big Steps wasn't the only company hit. That's our main company, but we have several subcompanies we've started over the years," I said.

"Jimmy, what are you saying?" I asked.

"Ross and I have been pouring over files all week. He had his hands in a couple of our subcompanies, but the PI did some digging of his own. You know Ace-Landic and Harold & Lace."

"You couldn't have thrown two more opposing companies at me," I said.

"I know, right? The PI acquired some of their balance sheets and financials as well, and he's been doing it to them too. The transactions. The small amounted debits. The altered final numbers. His initials. It's all there, Ashley."

I couldn't believe what I was hearing.

"I'm not going to lie, I didn't think Markus would've had multiple companies in his claws like this," I said. "How long has this been going on?"

"As far as we can tell, at least four years, but you're the one who figured out this was happening for all of my main company's life."

"And it's the same thing?" I asked.

"The same thing. Ross and I aren't sure if we can add to his charges already. And I'm not really sure if it'll make a difference."

"Why the hell wouldn't it make a difference?"

"With the charges he's already got on him, he'll lose everything before he gets out of jail. His company will sink, his reputation in the business field will be forever tarnished. No one will trust him with anything, and he'll come out close to penniless."

"Why does he even have to come out at all?" I asked.

"What good would that do?" he asked.

"This is a big thing, Jimmy. A massive, massive plan he's been building for years. That takes meticulous planning, manipulation, and a borderline psychopathic mind. Jimmy, don't you see that? He's hurt your subcompanies. And worse! Big Steps is paying for it. These other companies need to know what he's doing. This needs to get out there. If this is what he's done in the few years he spent in Miami, think about what he could've possibly done while he was in Alberta. It's possible this affects other countries, Jimmy."

"How could I have trusted a man like him?" he asked.

"He needs to pay for what he's done. All of it. And companies have a right to know his name so they can look at their own financials if they've ever come into contact with him. He's a con artist, Jimmy. He's a professional at swindling people. You can't beat yourself up over something like this."

"I know you're right. Ashley, look at me."

I looked into Jimmy's eyes and felt my heart skip a beat.

"I know you're right. About all of it. But what if I was saying all of this about your mother?"

"My mother wouldn't be capable of something like this."

"Not as you know her," he said. "That's the lens I was looking through with Markus. As I knew him, he wasn't capable of something like this. Ever. My world has been—"

I resisted the urge to reach out for his hand as he slammed it into the back of his head.

"He was a father figure to me, and he slapped me across my face," Jimmy said.

"Then use that anger," I said. "Use it to fuel the fire you need to turn him in."

"I can't do this without you, Ashley."

"Jimmy, you're stronger than this. You don't need me to hold your hand."

"Not to hold my hand, but to stand next to me. To guide me. You knew this. You saw this. And I was the idiot who didn't believe you. I fully own up to that, but I can't keep an unbiased opinion of my company and the people inside of it. You can."

"What are you asking me, Jimmy?"

"I want you back," he said. "But not only for me. For the company."

I reached out for my water and took a big gulp as he stared at me.

"I don't know, Jimmy."

"Will you let me prove it to you? Will you give me the chance to prove to you what's going on and how much this company needs you? How much I need you?"

"What did you say?" I asked.

"I need you, Ashley. Professionally and personally. Give me the chance to show you that. Even if you don't take your job back. Which is still on the table if you want it."

I felt my heart stop in my chest as I clutched my water in my hand.

"I don't know," I said.

"Just a chance. That's all I'm asking for," Jimmy said.

"You've thrown a lot at me."

"Then break it down into whatever you want. Whatever makes you happy, Ashley. That's what I want," he said. "But I don't think you're happy, and I want the chance to give you some of that happiness back."

I tossed my gaze out the window as his words settled into my head. My old job? An office down the hall from him? Back with the investors?

Back with Jimmy?

"Okay," I said.

"Okay to what?" he asked.

"I'll give you the chance to prove to me that you need me," I said. "But I still don't know about my job. I would like to take you up on the offer of talking Ross through all that stuff, though, should I choose not to take you up on your generous job offer."

"You deserve more than generous, but I'm willing to start with that," he said.

He held out his hand for us to shake on it, and I took it. Electricity shot up my arm, pressing goosebumps down my back. I held back the shiver shaking my legs as our hands moved up and down, my eyes locked on his. I missed his touch and the way my body came alive in his presence. I dropped his hand quickly and cleared my throat. Then, I picked my fork back up.

"So," I said. "What was I supposed to be consulting on?"

And the chuckle that fell from Jimmy's lips pulled a grin across mine.

Chapter 7

Jimmy

I was sitting at my desk combing through files on a Saturday that Ross told me needed a second look. Yet more proof that Markus was the lying asshole Ashley said he was. It made me sick. With the basic tallies Ross was able to do in the margins, even if the police dissolved all his accounts to pay back what he stole, we would still never get all the money back.

I shoved the files off to the side and raked my hands down my face.

A flash on my computer screen caught my attention. I toggled over to my email and saw I had something from Ashley. My hand began shaking as I opened it up, my mind going a thousand miles a second.

And I rejoiced when I read her words.

Mr. Sheldon,

I've given your job offer some thought, and I would enjoy coming back to my previous corporate position as Account Representative for the investors of Big Steps. But understand, this is strictly a business relationship.

Ashley Ternbeau

It was fucking better than nothing. Having her back at the company ensured our success. I shot her an email back, asking her if she wanted to go get dinner to hammer out the details of her reemployment, and her quick response back was a resounding no.

But when I promised her it would be strictly business since the company would be paying for the work dinner, she agreed.

I packed up the files and stuck them under Ross's door. I changed my shirt and tie in my office, and prepared to pick Ashley up at her place. I was shocked she had agreed to let me pick her up, but I was also glad.

Even though this was strictly professional, it would still feel like old times.

I drove to her apartment, and she was waiting outside for me. Her beautiful auburn hair was blowing in the wind, whipping around her gorgeous face. She was clutching her purse as her dress fluttered around her, a dress I hadn't seen on her yet.

It draped over her body fabulously, and it would make it hard to keep this professional.

"Thanks for picking me up," she said.

"I'm surprised you agreed to it," I said.

"One of my headlights is out, and with it getting darker, I would've surely been pulled over."

"Then I'm happy to assist. I would ask where you wanted to go, but the company does meetings at a restaurant that's known for its privacy," I said.

"Doesn't matter to me. Lead the way," she said.

We drove through town and pulled into the parking lot of the restaurant. It was one of the few places in Miami that had barred the media and paparazzi from its establishment. Any business dinner or clientele meeting initiated by myself was done at this place. The staff was paid well to keep their mouths shut, and unsavory characters usually weren't allowed inside.

It was the perfect place to talk to Ashley about her coming back to the company.

"So, a few things. I know you've been gone from the company for about a week and a half, but you're still going to see a regular paycheck," I said.

"Why?" Ashley asked.

"When you quit your job, my gut reaction was to find any way to get you back. You're a serious asset to my company, and you'll have a massive hand in righting the financial ship, so to speak. I cashed in some of your paid vacation days hoping I could convince you to come back."

"So I haven't technically even been terminated," she said.

"And you'll see no dock in pay."

"What would you have done had I not come back?"

"You would've seen regular paychecks for three months before official termination papers were mailed to you."

"Even with the severance package on the table?" she asked.

"The severance package wouldn't have been confirmed by me to be given out until the termination was processed."

"Okay. So, there's really nothing to discuss here."

"There is. Your office is still there. Do you want it?" I asked.

"I figured that was where I would be returning, yes."

"Because with our prior personal relationship, there are plenty of other offices on that floor that don't face me as well as offices on other floors with great views."

"That office will be fine, Jimmy."

"Okay. I wanted to make sure. Also, your perks. Using paid vacation time during this lapse means you're down to two and half weeks of paid leave, two weeks of paid medical leave, one week of unpaid medical leave, and one week of unpaid sick days. Is that still an okay deal? Or do you want to negotiate?"

"No, Jimmy. I don't want to negotiate," she said.

"You seem upset. What's wrong?"

"You really meant professional, didn't you?"

"Yes. I did."

I could see her professional facade cracking, and I wasn't sure how I felt about that.

"Fine. If we're keeping this absolutely professional, then I do have a bone to pick."

"Okay," I said. "What's wrong?"

"I figured out a billion-dollar lawsuit, and you treated me as if I had no idea what I was talking about. How do we go about figuring out how much respect I deserve in the office?"

"That's a fair question," I said. "What I can give you is a contract."

"A contract on respect."

"No. A contract outlining all the details we've spoken about. It'll outline all the areas that are deemed within your professional right to have expertise in. Ross has the same type of contract," I said.

"And what does this contract do?" she asked.

"In the event of something like this, where you're right and I'm wrong and I don't believe you're right, you can sue the company for any fallout that happens because of my inability to trust you."

"I can what?"

"When you quit your job, it was a direct result of the emotional turmoil because I didn't believe you. I didn't respect you as my corporate employee because I was viewing you through the lens of a personal relationship. This contract protects you from something like that happening again. I have one in place, Ross has one in place, so it's only fair you have one in place."

"Why didn't I have one in place before?" she asked.

"Because you were promoted quickly without going through the rigmarole we're going through now. Since you're coming back, we're going to do this right."

"Fine. That sounds good to me."

I grinned as her glass of wine was set in front of her. She was squirming, but she was trying not to make it look like she was. This was me in a professional environment, and she had never witnessed that before, not so personally and boldly. I could tell she was getting used to things, but I saw a glimmer in her eye that made me think she was second-guessing herself and this "strictly professional" relationship.

We ordered our food before I settled back into my chair. Ashley's eyes were attached to my chest, seemingly digesting everything I had thrown at her, but a movement behind her shoulder caught my stare.

And I felt the blood drain from my face.

"Jimmy, what is it?" Ashley asked.

My eyes connected with Nina as Ashley turned around.

This was the last thing I needed, running into this woman. I watched Ashley's back straighten as Nina's eyes danced between mine and Ashley's. I waited for her to approach us, to make some snarky comment I couldn't defend Ashley from because she was simply my employee now.

Instead of approaching us, she looked down and left the restaurant.

"Uh, what was that about?" Ashley asked.

"It looks like Ross's restraining order took," I said.

"Ross's what?"

"You've really been out of the loop."

"Seems like it. When did this happen? I thought she was in jail."

"She made bail and that was when Ross hopped on a restraining order. We had the manager from our date night and the manager from that night at the bar testify to her aggression, and I guess it worked."

"Well, I'm glad she's finally backing off you," she said.

"Me, too, Ashley. Me too."

"What else have I been out of the loop on?"

Her eyes looked up at me from beneath her lashes, and it tugged at my gut.

"Markus has tried to call me a few times from jail."

"Are you serious? Can he do that?" she asked.

"He can. He's allowed one phone call a day, and he apparently seems to keep making it me."

"Are you taking his calls?" she asked.

"I took the first one. I haven't taken any of them since. I'm not sure if I should, but a part of me wants to."

"Why?"

"Because I know what it feels like to have my calls not picked up by the one person I wish I could fix things with."

Our eyes connected before her beautiful green orbs fell to her wine.

"How's your mother doing, Ashley?"

"She's, um ... I mean, it's not pretty. But she's alive."

"That bad?" I asked.

"It's getting there. The nurses are already talking about switching her medication again, and this'll be the last time they can before she's beyond help."

"I'm sorry."

"I mean, people with Alzheimer's live six to eight years with it on average? She's put in seven. It's only a matter of time."

"That doesn't make it any easier."

"No," she said. "It doesn't."

A band on stage started to play, and I saw Ashley's eyes drift to them. A spark of happiness in the sadness that welled within her eyes happened, and I couldn't deny her what she wanted. I stood to my feet and offered her my hand, a grin sliding across my cheeks.

"A professional dance?" I asked.

"Is there such a thing?" she asked with a giggle.

"Wanna test the theory?" I asked.

She slipped her hand into mine, and I twirled her onto the floor. People started to watch us as her dress billowed out. I swayed her side to side and dipped her when the music called for it. The smile she had lit up her face as her hair whipped around her shoulders. The connection between us was growing. The anger in her eyes toward me was fading. Every time she turned into me, she allowed her body to step a little closer and allowed my hand to hold her a little lower on her back.

We were the only ones dancing, but I didn't care. Ashley was laughing and having a good time and that was all I cared about. We danced through three songs before I saw our food hit the table, so I twirled her out, and she took a bow for the crowd.

Everyone clapped for us as her cheeks reddened with embarrassment.

A slow number came on, and I pulled her into my body. Our food would need time to cool down, and a slow dance was the perfect way to give it room to breathe. My hand slid around her waist, and I pulled her close to me, her eyes gazing up into mine.

"Is this professional?" I asked.

"Nothing this fun is ever professional," she said. "But our food's gonna get cold."

"It's still steaming. Let's give it a chance to cool down."

"What if I want my steak piping hot?"

"You don't if you value your taste buds," I said.

The song ended, and I led her back to the table. We ate our food and talked like old times. Like nothing had ever taken place between us. The conversation flowed easily, and the laughter was bellyaching. My heart soared with every story she told me, and my spine shivered every time my foot passed hers underneath the table.

I paid for dinner, and I escorted her back out to my car. I opened her door, and she thanked me before sliding in with her delicate movements. I cranked up my car and gripped the steering wheel, but something stopped me.

I wasn't ready to take her home yet.

"I might be overstepping my boundaries," I said. "But is there any chance I could convince you to come back to my place for a drink?"

I looked over at the beautiful woman sitting next to me as she gazed up at the stars.

"I've always enjoyed the view from your apartment," she said. "I'm sure one drink won't hurt."

I was shocked she agreed, and I raced us back to my place. I promptly poured her a glass of wine that would complement the food she had eaten. She walked over to the towering windows at my place, and I turned on some mood music, draping the background with something we could listen to if she didn't want to talk.

"I spend way too much time on my porch at my place," Ashley said.

"There's no such thing as that," I said.

"I love the view. I love looking out over Miami and seeing everything from up above."

"Why?" I asked.

"It makes all of the problems and the quarrels seem less important."

I sipped on my bourbon as I turned toward her. She turned her eyes to mine, and I reached out for her body. She fell into me, her body pressing deeply as I wrapped my arm around her. We swayed to the slow rhythm of the music as the alcohol filled my stomach.

Her warmth was undeniable and comforting and familiar.

I missed this. I missed this connection with her. With the way she was looking up at me with her desire-soaked eyes told me she missed it, too, and she still felt between us what I was feeling. She finished her wine, and I took her glass from her, tossing the crystal onto the couch.

I'd clean it up in the morning.

"Ashley," I said.

"Just shut up and kiss me."

Her hand wrapped around the back of my head, and our lips collided. I pressed her against the glass and unraveled her hand from my head. Lacing our fingers together, I pinned her hand above her head, absorbing the press of her lips into me, her hips into me, her soul into mine.

I found her other hand and pinned it to the glass. My lips nipped at her cheek and traveled down her neck. She picked up her leg, wrapped it around me, and then jumped up to catch my hips between her thighs.

Even if this was my last moment with her, I would make sure it was one we would never forget.

I would make sure we ended on the best note I could possibly give her.

Chapter 8

Ashley

He carried me to his bedroom and slowly lowered me to the bed. Our lips connected in a sensual kiss as my hips undulated into him. I couldn't deny how much I wanted him and how good his body had felt against mine when we were dancing. I missed the connection we'd shared, that innate sense of knowing someone better than they thought. His lips traveled down my body as he undressed me, massaging every curve and kissing every crevice. I was on fire. My toes were curling as his lips streaked down my thighs. Electricity blinded my vision as his hands ran along my body, massaging my breasts, parting my thighs, and bending my knees to my chest.

His thick tongue ran along my slit, and I moaned. I arched into him, no longer trying to deny what I wanted. He kissed my pussy. Lapped at it. Swallowed the arousal that had built because of his touch. He pressed and licked and sucked as I rolled against him. My back arched, and my hands curled into the tendrils of his hair. I pulled him closer. Pressed him deeper. Allowed his name to drip from my lips.

"Jimmy. Jimmy. Yes. Right there. Right there."

He hummed in approval, and it sent me over the edge. My naked body shook and jumped as his tongue raked over my clit. I was dripping down to my ass, and he cleaned me up, licking from my ass to my pussy while I groaned at his wet warmth.

I looked down at him, and he peeked up between my legs. His eyes locked on mine as he lowered me back to the bed. He stood up and removed his clothes, taking his time as his chiseled form revealed itself to me.

I shook as he descended onto the bed.

His lips collided with mine, and my hands rushed to his hair. His hips fell between my legs as he guided himself into my body. I moaned. I wiggled. My legs trembled as I bit down on his lower lip. It was all too much, and yet it wasn't enough. The alcohol was heating my veins, and his muscles were twitching against my skin. He was rolling deeper than I'd ever felt him as his hand held my hips at an angle that made the room spin on its tilted axis.

I kissed him over and over, unable to get enough of his taste. The bourbon on his lips and the steak on his breath screamed "man" to me. My body was coming unhinged, bucking ravenously into him. My clit was pressing against his trimmed curls as my nails raked down his arms.

"Do it again," Jimmy said.

My eyes whipped open as our foreheads connected.

"I said do it again."

I reached around for his back and dug my nails in. I pressed deeply into his twitching muscles as he pounded into my hips, making my tits jump, and I raked his skin. Leaving red marks behind that welted as I chased what I wanted, what we both wanted.

"Ashley. Holy hell, I missed you."

His words sparked a fire in my chest as tears rose to my eyes.

I buried my face into the crook of his neck. I couldn't let him see me this vulnerable. My pussy throbbed around his cock, pulling him in deeper as he groaned. The bed rocked against the wall, the headboard crashing into the plaster. His body collapsed onto mine as his hands roamed my body, squeezing my breasts and tugging at my nipples, holding down my hips and massaging my thighs.

I couldn't get him close enough to me.

I sat us up and clung to Jimmy's body, straddled his lap. He held both of our bodies upright. I thrust against him shallowly, his dick pressing against that electric spot within my body. I shivered in his grasp, and I could feel him growing, pulsing against my walls as my juices dripping onto the bed.

I pressed open-mouthed kisses on his shoulder. Up his neck. On his cheek. Then our lips locked as my body burst.

I dug into his back as his arms covered mine. He pulled me into his body, arching me as he towered over my form. My hand rose up to his hair, wrapping my fingers in it as he exploded inside me. Thick threads of come shot deep into my body, painting me with his mark as I throbbed around him. I jolted with each electric shock that convulsed my muscles while his throat swallowed my moans.

"Oh, Jimmy," I said breathlessly. "Don't let go."

I was weak to the man who was Jimmy Sheldon. He held me close as his face fell to my neck, our bodies still connected at the hips. I gasped to catch my breath and root myself in reality as the room slowly stopped spinning.

I was shivering in his arms, and his muscles twitched against my skin.

Once I could see straight, I slid from his arms. I couldn't stay with him, even though he probably wanted me to. I gathered my clothes and got dressed, painfully aware that he was watching me.

It felt weird being in this position.

"I'll, um, see you Monday for work," I said.

"See you then, Ashley."

I walked to Jimmy's front door and left without looking back. I wanted to stay strong. I wished I could've stayed strong, but the pull between us was undeniable. I couldn't help it. I was in love with him, fully and completely, and the passion that flowed between us was an added bonus. I put my hand over my mouth as I walked to the elevator, leaving the man I loved behind in his room alone.

I wanted to go back and be with him, tell him how sorry I was and that things were okay.

But things weren't okay, not yet.

This didn't mean we were back together, and I had to make sure Jimmy knew that. Simply because we'd slept together didn't take that contract we'd talked about off the table. I would talk to him about it Monday during work hours. In his office with the door open.

Because I couldn't go back. If I did, I would stay, and I wasn't sure if that was the right move.

Chapter 9

Jimmy

"I have to say, we're a bit concerned by what happened during the last meeting."

"Are you planning on replacing Markus? Or will you be expecting us to foot his bill?"

"Have you looked into your other subcompanies? Were they affected as well?"

"I want to see the balance sheets from this month. I want to know this madness has been stopped."

"Where is Miss Ternbeau? I've been trying to get in contact with her for days about my investment."

My investors kept throwing tons of questions at me all at once without giving me a moment to speak up. I sat in my chair and let them bombard me as I tried to gather my thoughts. This was a hell of a way to start a Monday morning, especially after my encounter with Ashley the night before.

Fuck. It had been incredible.

"Mr. Sheldon, are you even listening?" Mr. Matthews asked.

"I am. I'm waiting for you all to hush so I can address your concerns," I said.

"Then, go ahead," he said. "Indulge us."

"What happened during the last meeting came as a shock to all of us, believe me. And yes, I plan on replacing Markus eventually. I have a few people who have expressed interest in being on the board in the past, so once I can get this mess cleaned up, I will be approaching them with numbers and valuations by the end of the month. As far as Miss Ternbeau goes, I've given her some time off. She was the one who brought all of this to my attention with Markus, and she was pretty badly shaken over it."

"Miss Ternbeau was the one who figured it out?" Mr. Matthews asked.

"Yes. Based off a conversation she had with him during one of our nightly outings," I said.

"Way to go," an investor said.

"She should be in here so we can thank her personally," another one said.

"And when she returns to work, you can all thank her. I'm sure she'll appreciate it. In the meantime, however, there is only one priority, and that is to clean up these balance sheets. Ross and I have combed through all our financials, and none of the withdrawals are taking place any longer. This month's balance sheet won't be clear because his arrest only took place a few days ago, but I've contacted our financial institutions, and they've put a stay on his account as well as his debits. Next month's balance sheets should be cleared, and I'll have them printed out week by week and put in a folder for you to have."

"When you say financials, do you mean Big Steps? Or all of your companies?" Mr. Matthews asked.

"All of my companies," I said. "I will get you the balance sheets for all of the companies."

"How will the money get returned to the company?"

"His immediate finances are being frozen and redirected. What we can prove immediately will be repaid over the next month. If anything else pops up during the investigation for any reason, then his assets will be liquidated to cover what he took," I said.

"Good. That man should pay up for what he stole from us."

"I'm doing everything I can to help the FBI with their investigation. They were brought in over the weekend to comb through everything, so don't let people in FBI jackets make you nervous. They're going to go through the subcompanies to make sure those are stable, but the more proof we can hand over on Markus, the better off we will be in court."

"Glad to hear it. If you need anything from us, you let us know," Mr. Matthews said.

Yeah. Except your investments.

I wasn't going to tell them that two of my subcompanies had been hit. I didn't have a big hand in them, but some of my investors did specifically invest in them as well. I was already on shaky ground as it was, and I knew divulging that information to them would upset them. The FBI was on my side with what to tell them and what not to. They knew two of my other companies had been hit. They were supportive that I wasn't ready to reveal the information, so I knew I could trust them not to open their mouths to the wrong people.

The investors seemed to be happy with my answers for the time being, which brought some temporary relief, but until I could get them investing again, we were going to have to tighten things around the office. I couldn't bank on that money that was supposed to be coming in from Markus's accounts. For all I knew, he had a fail-safe in place so no one could touch his "fortune." Since the clear balance sheets wouldn't come out until the end of next month, that meant we would go for the rest of this quarter without any other investments funneled into the accounts.

That would take a chunk out of our basic operations budget.

Fuck. This man had screwed me over. I dismissed the meeting, and the investors left, but I stayed seated in the room. Even with him being arrested, I was still having to clean up his damn mess.

My anger was boiling over again.

My phone rang in my pocket as Ross stepped into the empty room. I slid it out and took a look at it, half expecting to see Ashley's name. I wasn't sure how she would react to coming back to work after what happened between us over the weekend. Part of me was expecting her to quit and never come back.

Instead, it was my lawyer.

"Talk to me, Trish."

"Markus has been released from jail," she said.

"Are you fucking serious?" I asked.

"He posted his bail."

"His bail was set at fifty million dollars. He didn't have fifty million dollars."

"His girlfriend? Jamie? She has his power-of-attorney. She's already liquidating assets and emptying his accounts."

And there it was. The only way this situation could get worse.

"I thought his accounts were frozen," I said.

"His accounts. These accounts are in her name," Trish said.

"Of fucking course, they are."

"Look, he's innocent until proven guilty in this country. I know we have a lot of stuff on him proving his guilt, including the partial confession in the meeting last week, but he still has to be convicted by a jury of his peers. If he had the money to post his bail, they have to let him go," she said.

"How the fuck is this man constantly wiggling his way out of things?" I asked.

"We'll get him. Look, Jimmy, I'm in the process of setting up a meeting between me and my team and Markus's team. I'm sure they'll be looking for some sort of a deal, but I have a plan."

"You want to get him to confess to the subcompanies," I said.

"I think we can. If we can get his confession like we did last time, even if it's a roundabout one, it takes any possible deal off the table."

"Why?"

"Because it proves premeditated thought. Right now, they're working under the assumption that he saw an opportunity and jumped. Doing this to other companies brings premeditation into the picture, and that's rough going in a court of law."

"When can you get this meeting on the books?" I asked.

"Since I'm as good as I say I am, after lunch today."

"Great. You tell them they're coming here," I said. "We'll meet in the investor's conference room."

"I'll let them know," she said.

I hung up the phone, and Ross tossed some food in front of me. I grimaced and pushed it away before he sat a coffee down in front of me as well. We ate in silence as the people in FBI jackets kept hauling boxes of shit out, and every time they stuck their heads in, I wanted to punch one of them in the throat.

I didn't know how I was ever going to recuperate from this mess.

"You want to talk about Ashley being back?" Ross asked.

"Is she in today?" I asked.

"No. She called and said to let you know she would officially be starting tomorrow. She said she expected a contract on her desk so she could sign it."

"It's already there," I said.

"So it's true. She's coming back."

"She is."

"That's great. We're going to need her for all of this. You think she would testify against Markus?"

"One step at a time, but I'm pretty sure she would enjoy that," I said.

"What contract is she talking about?"

"The one you and I signed with one another. You know, the 'I respect your opinion and expertise' contract."

"She didn't have one of those before?"

I shot him a look as I finished my sandwich.

I got a message from my lawyer saying she was headed this way for the meeting. I went to my office to clean myself up and then got all of the FBI guys off the floor. I didn't want anything deterring Markus from telling us the truth. I gathered the evidence Ross and I found with my subcompanies and pushed it into a folder. Then the two of us sat and waited for everyone.

Trish walked in a few minutes before one, and by one thirty, I was looking at him.

The mangy asshole who was in the process of ruining me.

"Any questions you have will be addressed to me," Markus's lawyer said. "I'm Peter."

"Don't worry. I won't do much talking," I said.

"My client won't be speaking much either," Trish said as she shot me a look.

I passed her the folder, and she grinned at me.

"I'll make this short and sweet. I'm here to discuss a plea bargain," Peter said.

"Not going to happen," Trish said.

"My client is willing to admit to where he stashed the money he took in exchange for a reduced sentence," Peter said.

"So your client does admit to stealing the money," Trish said.

"Yes, and he is remorseful for that theft," Peter said.

"I'm sure he is. What is a 'reduced sentence'?" Trish asked.

"Five years in a prison in Canada so he can be near his family and then one year in house arrest," Peter said.

"You've got to be kidding me. Your client's looking at ten plus years in prison," Trish said.

"And your client is out millions of dollars I'm sure he'd like to see again," Peter said.

"I'm not admitting to anything," Markus said.

"What was that?" I asked.

"I'm not admitting to anything until the plea bargain keeps me out of jail," Markus said.

"Markus, hush," Peter said.

"You're going to jail," I said. "And you're going to rot."

"Jimmy, enough," Trish said.

"I just got out of jail, and I have no intention of going back. I'm willing to hand it all over. Every single penny of the twenty million I stole, but I'm not going back to prison. House arrest for the ten years I'm supposed to spend in prison. That's the plea bargain," Markus said.

He looked over at his lawyer, and I watched Peter sigh.

"That's the plea bargain," Peter said.

"It's still a no," Trish said.

"I'm not guilty," Markus said. "You have some stories and a few initials on some paper."

"So you're willing to hand over money you say you have, but you didn't take it," I said. "You're not very good at this, are you?"

I watched Trish push the folder over to Markus's lawyer. I grinned at her as she relaxed in her chair. Peter flipped the folder open, and his eyes widened. I watched Markus lean over and look at it as his face paled.

We had them right where we wanted them.

"We know you're guilty," Trish said. "You weren't only dipping into Big Steps, you were dipping into Jimmy's other companies. From the tallies we've made so far, you took twenty million from Big Steps and a total of nine million between both of these sub-companies."

I watched Markus's jaw clench as his eyes darted over to his exasperated lawyer.

"Right now, this hasn't been submitted. The FBI doesn't know about it, and we can keep it that way," Trish said.

"For what price?" Peter asked.

"We want a clear admission to what Markus stole," Trish said.

"He'll give the money back. We've already established that," Peter said.

"He's not getting out of this. That man manipulated my client for years. He had his hands in this company from the very beginning. Your client is a con artist and a psychopath, and he doesn't deserve to be walking around with the rest of us. Mr. Sheldon will get his money.

Once your client's convicted in front of a jury, they will liquidate everything to pay Mr. Sheldon back. That's our offer. We don't bring up the new charges if you admit guilt to the ones already filed. That's the only deal you're getting," Trish said.

Markus and Peter started talking. I looked over at Ross, and he made a motion to try and tell me to shove my anger down. What did Markus think he was getting out of all of this? He was going to jail. He wasn't going to get off scot-free after stealing millions of dollars from my companies.

"The original plea bargain still stands," Peter said.

"I take it that's a 'no' to our offer," Trish said.

"Yes, it is."

"Then we will be turning this evidence over to the FBI within forty-eight hours. Enjoy American prison, Markus. It's not a cozy as Canada," Trish said.

I dismissed Markus from the table with a wave of my hand. Peter got up and tried to lead Markus to the door, but he stopped and turned his head. The smile that grew on his face was frightening. It didn't quite meet his eyes. I held his gaze even though I felt the blood draining from my face.

This wasn't the smile of the man I'd come to know and love. This was the smile of a completely different person.

"I know you won't hand it over," Markus said.

"Markus, stop it," Peter said.

"I won't be sent back to jail," Markus said.

"Get out of the room now," Peter said.

"My lawyer will find a way to keep me out of jail. I've got plans in place you couldn't dream of, Jimmy. You thought I was mentoring you, but you were the biggest pawn of them all."

"Let's go!" Peter said.

His lawyer practically shoved him out of the room as I stood to my feet.

I watched them make their way for the elevator as Markus rolled his shoulders back. I looked over at Ross, and his jaw was hanging in shock. I felt so many conflicting emotions, but none of them more than emptiness.

The relationship I had built with that man for twelve years was nothing but an enormous lie.

"Jimmy, we need to talk about—"

I pushed past Trish and rushed to my office. I needed to be alone. To think and decompress. I locked my office door and turned off all the lights. I sat down in my leather chair and turned toward the Miami coastal view and then put my hands over my mouth.

Markus would've told me it was weak for a businessman to shed tears, but Markus had been a lie.

So wasn't his advice a lie too?

Chapter 10

Ashley

I was officially back at work, but people were talking. Rumors were flying about why I hadn't been in the office and why I was suddenly back. Some people thought I was sick, and other people thought I was helping Markus. Some people were developing rumors that I was screwing my boss to keep my job. I ignored them and kept walking to my office, trying to shake off the insanity around the office.

I wanted to look out over all of Miami and settle my soul down.

I had to take this job back. I didn't have a choice. I needed the money for my mother and my bills, and no one else was hiring me. I set my stuff down on my desk and picked up the contract, looking it over before I signed it.

I walked it over to Jimmy's office and slid it under his door, trying to ignore the snickers and huffs coming from every direction.

I sat at my desk and got to work. I went through and balanced the investor's accounts and answered their endless emails. I apologized for my absence and sent off the PDF documents forecasting the growth of their investments even with the looming investigation. It was going to hit the media eventually. There was always that one person who couldn't keep their mouth shut. I made sure to include all the ugly details, no matter how upsetting they were to the investors.

That was what they enjoyed the most. My honesty instead of my coaxing.

There were some random things that had been dropped into my company mailbox, receipts and transactions to double-check and payroll things to go over. Everyone was apparently paranoid about all their calculations with Markus kicking things up. So they all wanted me to go over their final numbers to make sure everything was right.

I hunched over my desk and ran the numbers in my head until a knock came at my door.

"Miss Ternbeau?"

I lifted my head and saw a man standing at my door, tall and lanky with disheveled hair and a gun on his hip. He flashed his FBI badge, and I ushered him in, sitting back in my chair.

"Not here. We were wondering if you could meet us in Mr. Sheldon's office?" he asked.

"Uh, sure. Yeah. Give me a second to lock all of this down, and I'll be in there," I said.

What was going on? Why did I have to be in Jimmy's office for this? Were we in trouble for something? I locked my office door behind me and headed to Jimmy's office. The door was shut promptly behind me when I entered.

I looked up at Jimmy for the first time since our encounter, and he seemed heavy with burden.

What in the world had happened?

"Would you like to have a seat, Miss Ternbeau?"

"No. I want you to tell me why I'm in my boss's office when he looks like he's just been run through a meat grinder," I said.

"All we want you to do is tell us everything you know about Markus Bryant," the agent said.

"We couldn't have done this in my office?" I asked.

"Ashley, please," Jimmy said.

I whipped my head over to him and watched him lean into his chair.

"Fine. I know Markus is guilty of all this," I said.

"How so?" the agent asked.

"It all fits. Lou Roth is LR."

"Who's Lou Roth?"

"Markus's mother has Alzheimer's. Had Alzheimer's. Whatever. Lou is Markus's middle name and also a name she used to call him whenever she mistook him for his father. Roth was his mother's maiden name. She would constantly correct the nurses on her name if she couldn't remember that she'd gotten married," I said.

"Okay. How do the rest of the dots connect?" the agent asked.

"Isn't this your job?" I asked.

"Please, Miss Ternbeau."

"Fine. There are no initials on balance sheets for the first three years of the company, which coincides with when Markus moved his company headquarters to Canada. Jimmy has openly admitted to giving financial control over to Markus a few times during the beginning stages of his company, so Markus could've laid some sort of subset equation or recurring transaction into the software we use for the company," I said.

"What if the software's been changed?"

"It hasn't. The hardware has, and the software's been upgraded but not changed."

"How do you know that?"

"Because I went down to the damn IT department and asked questions," I said.

I saw Jimmy grinning from the corner of my eye. This was ridiculous and a waste of my time. I had people in this company accusing me of fucking my way to the top, I had investors who were having mild panic attacks in my inbox, and everyone on this forsaken planet wanted me to double-check their damn numbers.

Now, I was having to tell this story again?

"Miss Ternbeau, would you be willing to go on the stand as a witness?" the agent asked.

"I'll be cooperative in whatever efforts you pursue," I said. "Is that all you needed?"

"Yes, ma'am."

"Then lead with that next time," I said.

The agent snickered and shook his head before he left the office. I started to leave as well before Ross slipped in and closed the door. He whipped around and held out a folder for me, and I groaned and rolled my eyes.

"Nice to have you back," Ross said.

"Why can't I be in my own office?" I asked.

"Just take a look," he said.

"What is that?" Jimmy asked.

"I did some digging into those so-called random companies. Ace-Landic and Harold & Lace. You'll never guess what I found," Ross said.

"You've invested into some of their projects," I said.

"We've what?" Jimmy asked.

"It's right here," I said. "Ace-Landic's clean energy project four years ago and H&L's—what is that?" I asked.

"What the hell is a 'party dildo'?" Jimmy asked.

"Beats me. I gave them a call to figure out what was going on, and you'll never guess what they told me."

"Spit it out," I said.

"Oh, someone's terse," Ross said. "Anyway, they did confirm we invested in their projects. Not much, only like one hundred thousand dollars. But guess who negotiated on your behalf?"

"No fucking way," I said.

"Fucking forged your signature and everything. I had them fax over the paperwork. It's the last couple of pages," Ross said.

"Oh my gosh. Jimmy, that looks exactly like your signature," I said.

"He's a con artist to the max," Ross said. "He's also a short-term player on both of their investment boards."

"Have you turned this over to the FBI yet?" Jimmy asked.

"You need to if you haven't," I said.

"Not yet. I want to make sure I have every single shred of evidence to put this man away for a long time," Ross said. "But I also don't want the media finding out."

"You and me both," Jimmy said.

"You need to call the FBI agent guy back into this office," I said. "Or at least get your lawyer over here."

"Don't worry, we are many steps ahead of you," Jimmy said.

"Oh? Then enlighten me," I said.

"We had a meeting yesterday with Markus and his lawyer that went better than most realize," Jimmy said.

"Really? It went better," Ross said.

"Markus practically unveiled his plan. He isn't going to jail, which means he's a flight risk. Half of his accounts are in Jamie's name and half of them are probably in his. This is the missing link we were looking for. His personality switched on a dime, Ashley. He gave me this smile that didn't quite reach his eyes and started talking about how he thought I wouldn't hand over information to the authorities and how his lawyer was going to keep him out of jail. But they made one mistake," Jimmy said.

"What was that?" I asked.

"They didn't ask Ross to leave the room," Jimmy said.

"I don't follow."

"I can be used as a witness on the stand to that meeting because the charges are Sheldon vs. Bryant. Not Big Steps," Ross said.

"Oh. That's good. That's a really smart move," I said.

"I'm going to call my lawyer and see what else can be done, but we're gonna nail this asshole to the wall. This will throw out any chance he's got at a plea bargain, and he'll be back at square one legally," Jimmy said.

"I'm proud of you, Jimmy."

His eyes fell to me, and I watched them soften.

"I'm glad you're doing the right thing," I said. "I know you still feel guilty for turning him in, but you're about to save more companies than just your own."

"I know," he said. "That's really the only thing pushing me forward right now."

"Should I leave the two of you alone?" Ross asked.

"No," I said. "I have a lot of work to get back to. Keep me in the loop. Jimmy, did you get that contract I signed?"

"Stepped on it this morning," he said.

"Good. Let me know if you need anything."

As I walked back to my office, I was painfully aware of how people were still gossiping. They were giggling and pointing and grimacing as I walked by. If they were trying to be subtle, it wasn't working very well. Being that close to Jimmy after our encounter over the weekend should've been hard. It should've been tense and terse and all sorts of things.

What it shouldn't have been was wanted. What it shouldn't have been was craved.

I sat down at my desk and started wondering if we could be together through all this shit. With the office talking, if we ever did strike up something again, it wouldn't be the same. With the media sure to get their hands on what was going on, it was only a matter of time before our prior relationship was revealed.

Could we really try to strike it up again during all this bullshit?

I didn't know, and I couldn't dwell on it. I sunk my teeth back into the work on my desk and tried to keep Jimmy out of my mind. But every time I looked up and saw his office, his door was open. I could see him sitting at his desk, working away like I was.

Every once in a while, he would look up and catch me staring.

Shit. This wasn't a good decision.

We weren't going to make it.

Chapter 11

Jimmy

I knew I needed to call my lawyer, but I wasn't sure if I really wanted to or even if I could. Should I call the FBI investigator first? Should I bypass my lawyer altogether? Was it possible for us to tack on any more charges? It was wrong to keep this information to myself, and I needed to be doing what Ashley was suggesting. It wasn't possible for Markus to do something like this and have ever cared about me.

That truth hurt in a place I hadn't touched in decades.

I was a lost little boy again, digging through the trash and finding scraps for my mother to eat. I was staring in the face of my alcoholic father, his smile lopsided as puke poured from the side of his mouth. I was that little boy again, huddled beneath a tarp I'd found for my mother and me to take shelter from the rainstorms battering our hometown.

Markus had stranded me.

The man I had chosen to be my father stranded me like my real father had.

My heart hurt so much I couldn't breathe. I leaned over and tried to catch my breath as a tear dripped off my nose. It felt like a thousand sharpened daggers were plunging into my skin, robbing me of the very life I once enjoyed living.

I drew in deep breaths, trying to calm the pain coursing through my body.

Ashley was right. I knew in my rational mind she was right and I was wrong. I had to hand over this information. I had to throw as much of it at them as I could. Markus was a con artist. It was his job to trick people into having deep, intimate relationships with them. For all I knew, Jamie was a pawn as well, a girlfriend he would strand in the cold the moment she was no longer convenient for him. I turned my chair around and wiped at my face. I flipped the folder open Ross had given me and stared down at the papers.

Markus had invested on behalf of my company, weaseled his way into these companies and stolen from them. He'd used my fucking signature to do it.

I shoved the file away and turned my attention to my email. I toggled my mouse and was met with a blinding flashing light. There were scores of unanswered emails from all sorts of news outlets. Fox. CNN. Tabloid magazines. People. Times. Local newspapers. And they were all wondering the same thing.

They were all wondering why Ashley was fired and brought back.

Why the hell did that matter? And who the fuck told them Ashley had been fired? There were no termination papers. I had never filed anything with HR on it. The only thing I had was the email in my inbox saying she wasn't returning to work.

Holy shit, had someone hacked into my fucking inbox?

I searched my name on the internet and got tons of articles, all published between last night and this morning. "Big Kahuna Bangs Little Fish." "Sheldon And Ternbeau, Sitting In A Tree." "Sexual Harassment On The Horizon For Big Steps?"

My vision was dripping red as I combed through the articles.

There were allegations of sexual harassment charges and lawsuits in the making. There were allegations of us screwing in my office and using company funds for dates. There were allegations of me giving Ashley her job back because she agreed to suck my dick under my desk four nights a fucking week.

I slammed my chair out from behind my desk and walked out into the hallway.

I caught Ashley coming in for the day, and I pulled her directly into my office. I looked around and made sure the coast was clear before I shut the door. There were tears in her eyes, which told me she already knew what was going on. Her phone was probably flooded with all sorts of disgusting headlines from various online "sources."

"I'm so embarrassed," Ashley said. "I never should've come back."

"You had every right to. You're more than qualified for the position," I said.

"Cass called me this morning in an absolute frenzy. I didn't even know what she was talking about until I scrolled through the messages she sent me last night."

"Ashley, look at me."

"I can't," she said.

"Please."

Her beautiful green eyes fluttered up at me. The pain coursing through them dealt the final blow to my gut. I couldn't help myself. I wrapped her up in my arms and pulled her close and was shocked when she allowed me to do so. She cried into my chest, sniffling and hiccupping as her shoulders shook.

"I'm going to hold a press conference this afternoon and clear this all up," I said.

"They won't listen. They never do with stuff like this," Ashley said.

"I'll make them believe me like they did with the social media scandal," I said.

"I'm not going to be there for it. I can't stand there and watch you this time."

"You're not going to, even if you wanted to. You'll be in your office working like the corporate woman you are."

"What are we going to do?" she asked.

Just hearing her say the word "we" sent my heart fluttering with hope.

"I'm going to call this press conference, and you're going to work. Don't let anyone into your office except Ross. He'll be our go-to communications guy. If you need me, pick up your office phone and call me that way," I said.

"Okay. I can do that."

I got on the phone with the PR department downstairs and had them set up a press conference for four in the afternoon. I wanted to make a statement and then get the fuck home. I had my security team scanning through the systems trying to figure out if someone had hacked into my email and saw that message from Ashley.

Because the only other explanation was speculation, which meant someone in my company was opening their damn mouth.

I put on my best suit in my office and then started downstairs. I looked over toward Ashley's office to try and see her, but her door was closed, which was probably for the best anyway. I sent my receptionist home early so she could beat the traffic that would ensue after this statement was over. Then I made my way downstairs.

"Ladies and gentlemen, I'm here to address some rumors flying around. I won't be taking any questions because I'm pretty sure all the nasty articles flying around center around one topic. Ashley Ternbeau and I have not been together in my office. There's no sex on a desk or any sort of derogatory agreement where she obtained her job in exchange for sexual favors. She was never fired, and there are no sexual harassment lawsuits pending against me. I was going to have Miss Ternbeau work from a potential new location my company was about to open, but things fell through when we found fraud within Big Steps."

I watched all the reports eyes bug at the mention of fraud.

"Mr. Sheldon, what do you mean by fraud?"

"Is someone stealing from your company?"

"Is that why there are unmarked police vehicles spotted coming and going from your office?"

"Do you have any leads as to who's committing this fraud you speak of?"

"I told you I would not take any questions. An investigation is underway, and I promise you, it will wet your palette for drama. But it's not okay to take a valued member of my corporate team and slaughter her reputation in the media simply because she's a woman. If Miss Ternbeau were 'Mr. Ternbeau,' this would not be happening. There would be no wondering if 'Mr. Ternbeau' screwed his way to the top. Miss Ternbeau has an incredible IQ, can compute complex mathematical equations without ever pulling out a pen, she can speed read, she's a wonderful customer interface, and she has single-handedly reorganized the way I do my financials. If anything, my company is better because of her."

"The fraud, Mr. Sheldon. What about the fraud?"

"Miss Ternbeau was never fired, and there are no harassment lawsuits because no harassment has taken place," I said.

"But what about the fraud?"

"What can you tell us about that?"

"Is it someone from inside your company?"

"On your investor's board?"

"What does Mr. Fowler think about this? Does he know?"

"I'm not able to answer questions about the ongoing investigation at the moment. Thank you for your time," I said.

Then I stepped offstage and made my way back into my office.

The cameras were flashing, and people were trying to follow me. My security team was keeping the hounds at bay. Traffic was being directed so my employees could get out of the parking garage and go home to their families, and part of me thought about shutting down the entire company for the next few days. The heat was strong, and announcing the investigation would make both my lawyer and the FBI irate.

But it took the heat off Ashley, and that was all I wanted.

I went back to my office and looked down at the crowd below. My security team was still struggling to get everyone off the sidewalk. The building was quickly emptying of the people who had been loyal to me for so many years. I looked over at Ashley's office and saw that she had locked up and gone home for the day. I reached over and refreshed my screen, waiting for all the headlines about sexual harassment and Ashley to disappear.

Then, after fifteen minutes of refreshing my screen, I saw the first headline.

'Fraud At Big Steps. Who's To Blame?'

And Ashley's name wasn't mentioned once.

Chapter 12

Ashley

I pulled into work the next day and was shocked to see so many journalists and paparazzi standing outside the building. I pushed my sunglasses up onto my face and steadied myself into the parking garage as the company's security worked them back from the opening garage. It was insane, what they were trying to do to get information. It sickened me in a way. This company had been through enough. Jimmy had been through enough. All of us had been through enough over the past few months.

Why couldn't everyone back off?

I snuck out of my office the moment Jimmy had left for the press conference. I rushed to get out of the building before any of it started. I listened to it on the radio during my ride home and almost slammed into a light pole when he mentioned the fraud.

I couldn't believe he'd dropped that bomb to the media on his own, but it didn't stop people from approaching me.

"Miss Ternbeau?"

I whipped around in the parking garage and found someone with a microphone coming at me.

"Miss Ternbeau, if we could have a moment of your time."

I picked up the pace of my walking as the elevator came into view. Two more people came out of the shadows with microphones and cameras. They were asking me questions about how long Jimmy and I had been sleeping together, and if having a relationship with him affected our working relationship. They threw questions like "how long have you been together?" and "what's it like screwing your boss?"

I pressed my fingers on the elevator buttons, trying to keep my cool as security men came around the corner.

"Hey! Hey! What the hell are you guys doing down here?"

The press took off, running with their microphones and their cameras as the burly men chased them down and arrested them.

I got into the elevator and squeezed my eyes shut. I was questioning things more than ever. How could our relationship work with all this chaos around us? How in the world were we supposed to keep this under wraps now? How were we supposed to start over and try to get this off the ground if people were hounding us about allegations that were technically true?

If this was even something I wanted to start up again.

There were times when it felt right and times when it didn't. Yesterday, when I was walking into work, it felt right. Falling into Jimmy's arms and crying felt right. Leaning into his comfort felt right. But as I rode up the elevator all the way to the top floor, it no longer felt right. It no longer felt comfortable and safe.

Yes, we'd gone out and had a nice time. Yes, we'd hooked up this weekend. That didn't mean our issues were actually fixed. We hadn't magically sorted through all the turmoil we'd put one another through for the past two days. What happened between us didn't mean I trusted Jimmy or that he trusted me, and it didn't mean I felt safe talking to him or confiding in him about things.

Hell, I couldn't even go into his office professionally with everyone breathing down our neck. How were we supposed to fix what was so broken between us if everyone was watching our every move?

I headed to my office and tried to hold my head as high as I could. People were still staring and snickering behind my back, but the key was to show them it didn't affect me. If I gave in to the pressure, it assumed guilt, and that was the last thing either of us needed. But I was curious as to who was feeding the press this in the first place.

I set my stuff down at my desk and flopped into my chair. Instantly, I got back up to shut my door, closing out the prying eyes and the ears trained on me. I picked up my phone, perched on the corner of my desk, and then dialed Jimmy's office number.

He picked up immediately and apologized.

"I got wind of what happened in the parking garage. They've been arrested and charged with felony trespassing," Jimmy said.

"It's okay. I mean, we didn't think it was going to completely go away, right?" I asked.

"Honestly? That was the plan."

"Then it was a terrible plan," I said.

"Did you have a good morning otherwise?" he asked.

I snickered and shook my head as I slid from the desk into my seat.

"It was what it was. Cass stayed with me last night in case people figured out where I lived. I told them they weren't that crazy, but with them in the parking garage, now I'm not so sure," I said.

"If they show up at your apartment, you need to do two things. You need to call the police, and then you need to call me," he said.

"Done and done. Have you called your lawyer yet? You know, about the other companies?" I asked.

"I haven't, but I've sort of been busy with something else."

"Jimmy."

"My lawyer's working on this company right now. Big Steps. That's what matters right now. My subcompanies will bounce back. Ace-Landic and H&L will be informed via the FBI once they dig up the information on their own if they haven't already dug it up. But Big Steps is going to have a very bad quarter if we don't see any of that money within the next month or so. I have my lawyer sorting that out first."

"You need to hand this over, Jimmy. It's bothering me that you still aren't," I said.

"Why?" he asked.

"Because it feels like you're still protecting him despite all he's done and all he's tried to ruin and swindle multiple companies out of."

"Then I'll call my lawyer at lunch."

"It needs to be done now, Jimmy, especially since you dropped that bomb in the media yesterday. They know about the fraud. Investigative journalists will dig this up. And if they come clean with it before you do, what's that going to make you look like to them?"

"Can you hold on, Ashley? One of the investigators is calling me on my cell phone."

"I'll be right here," I said.

I could hear Jimmy talking on the other end, but I couldn't figure out what he was saying. All I could tell was that his words were getting more and more exasperated. Whatever the investigator had to say, things weren't good.

I really hoped Jimmy was coming clean with them about what we'd found a couple of days ago.

"You still there?" Jimmy asked.

"What was that about?"

"Just ... so much," he said.

"Did you tell them?"

"I told you, I'm going to tell my lawyer at lunch. We're getting lunch, and then she'll know. But I have to cut this call short, unfortunately. The investigators are heading my way for another meeting."

"Do you want someone there?" I asked.

"Are you offering?"

Was I offering? And if I was, then why was I offering? I leaned back into my chair and listened to Jimmy's steady breathing. I closed my eyes and reminisced on the better days when we could go to a restaurant and dance in one another's arms without quizzical eyes and prying media outlets, when we partied at the hotel and when he took me up to his room.

I thought back to our first night together and how hot his touch had been against my body.

I cared for him.

Even though I wasn't sure we could make it work, it didn't stop me from caring.

"I am, but it's probably not a good look," I said.

"I was thinking the same thing. Want me to call you when it's over?" Jimmy asked.

"Sounds good. I'll be here," I said.

I hung up the phone and tried to distract myself with work, monotonous and boring, and I didn't bother getting up to try and get lunch. I worked straight through and didn't leave my office for any reason. Partially because I didn't want to face the crowd outside for food and partially because I didn't want to face the office building.

I also didn't want to risk missing Jimmy's phone call.

The second my phone rang, I yanked it off the receiver. I took a deep breath and put it to my ear, but I could feel the tension seeping through the phone.

"Ashley Ternbeau."

"It's me," Jimmy said.

"I take it the meeting didn't go well," I said.

"A nice chastisement for what I pulled yesterday, but I had my reasons," he said.

"So you didn't tell them about the documents," I said. "Did you tell your lawyer over lunch?"

I heard the grandiose sigh fill the phone, and I shook my head. I was worried about Jimmy, very worried. Even as a young man, I wasn't sure how much more of this his body could take. The stress was wearing him down like it had worn me down in the beginning before I set this chain of events in motion. He had bags underneath his eyes he was trying to conceal, and he was talking a little slower than normal. His breath constantly smelled of coffee whenever I was around him, and his stance seemed a little crooked at times.

It was faint, but if someone knew Jimmy Sheldon well enough, they could see the pressure getting to him.

"Take Friday off," I said.

"You the boss now?" Jimmy asked.

"Take a long weekend. You can't handle this any longer. You need to find a way to decompress."

"And what about you?" he asked.

"What about me?"

"Are you coming to decompress with me?"

"Seriously? With all these rumors flying around?"

"I have enough money to keep us hidden for a long weekend, Ashley. If I need to unwind, then you really need to unwind, both professionally and personally."

"Jimmy, that's not a smart idea," I said.

"I'm not going unless you come with me."

"You're being stubborn."

"No one helps me decompress better than you do. Your presence is comforting, and your voice is like a medicine ball for my ears. If you think a long weekend is what I need, and you want me to use my time as wisely as possible, then I need all my tools at my disposal."

"So I'm a tool," I said with a grin.

"You're whatever you want to be. You're that kind of woman. But I think a long weekend away would do us both some good. Like I said, both personally and professionally."

"Talking about our relationship is not even close to decompressing," I said.

"Do we still have a relationship?" he asked.

The phone call went silent, and I closed my eyes. Even though I knew it was a terrible idea and even though the logical side of my mind was telling me to stand my ground, I wanted to go. I wanted to be with Jimmy. I wanted to hide away for a few days and sleep in his arms and enjoy his presence. Maybe that was what we needed to get us back on track. Maybe we needed a few uninterrupted days to simply be us.

But his question was important. Did we still have a relationship?

"I guess we should figure that out this weekend, huh?" I asked.
"I'll make the arrangements and give you a call," Jimmy said.

Chapter 13

Jimmy

I picked up the phone in my office and dialed Ashley's number. Sitting back in my seat, a massive smile crossed my face. This was happening. I was getting alone time with Ashley after everything that had happened. This was my chance to prove to her I was the man she thought I was, that I could treat her the way she deserved to be treated and that we could get through this. I kept my eyes trained on my office door in case anyone wanted to come barging in on me, and I smiled as her voice graced my ears.

"Ashley Ternbeau's office."

"You sound out of breath," I said.

"I was in the bathroom. Sorry," she said.

"No need to be sorry. I wanted to let you know I went ahead and made the arrangements."

"Wonderful. That's-that's great. What, um, are the plans?"

"You're cute when you stutter, you know that?" I asked.

"Already laying it on thick, I see."

"I have a lot to make up for," I said.

"So what's the plan?"

"I'm going to go ahead and leave my office. I've already informed Ross as well as the FBI that I'm not fleeing any scene. Merely taking some time to myself since I don't feel well from the stress of this situation."

"You do sound terrible."

"Compliment taken," I said. "I have a private beach house with a private section of the beach no one is allowed on but me. Miles away from civilization, but close enough to where if something melts down, I can get here if needed."

"So, right outside Miami?"

"Yep."

"How do you want to handle us leaving? I'm assuming it'll have to be some fancy maneuvering."

"Not really. I'm going to leave now, and you leave at the end of your day. Finish the work you have on your plate, but don't stay any later than four. Go home and pack a few things. A bikini. A dress."

"You think I own a bikini?"

"A bra and panties will do fine," I said with a grin.

"Oh, you're bad."

"I always try to be. Something to swim in and two outfits to change into is all you'll need. I've got toiletries there I'm sure you can use."

"Okay. Where do I go from there?" she asked.

"That coffee shop down the street from your apartment. It sits on an alleyway."

"You want me to wait for you in an alleyway?" she asked.

"No. I'll be coming down that alleyway to pick you up. The coffee shop has a side door. I'll text you when I'm there, you can come out and get in, and then we'll use the backroads to get to my beach house."

"I don't like this sneaking around."

"If you don't want to go, you don't have to. But I'm hoping you'll stick this out with me and come along. You could use the downtime as well, and selfishly, I'd like a chance to show you I'm not the man you think I am."

The silence on the phone gripped my throat. I was scared she was going to back out. Say no and destroy all the plans I already had in motion. I had a bottle of wine chilling for us and a beautiful sunset calling our name. I had a California king-sized bed for us to muss up and a walk-in shower for me to take her in.

If she would let me.

"Okay," she said. "I'll message you when I'm at my apartment."

"Good. I'm heading out. I'll see you soon."

I passed by one of the FBI officers and made sure I informed them one last time as to where I was going and what I was doing. I didn't want there to be any surprises or any suspicions as to the fact that I was fleeing anything. At that point, I had no idea what the hell Markus had roped this company into. For all I knew, he was working everything to make it look like it was my fucking fault. The man I didn't think was capable of stealing from me was quickly turning into a massive con artist.

It was unsettling, to say the least.

I didn't want to make anyone upset or make them think I was guilty of anything, but Ashley had been right. I needed a day off, away from all this bullshit. I got down to my car, having given my driver a couple of days off, and headed back to my apartment. I packed a small bag and made sure things were okay at the company with Ross before heading down to my Jaguar.

Ashley's message came through as I was closing the trunk of my car.

I kept to the back roads and tried to stay off the main drag. The press were everywhere, and I wasn't ready for one of them to start tailing me. They were still picketing outside the office, and a couple of them had been found at the entrance of the lobby of my apartment. Of course, they were arrested for stuff like that. My apartment complex had a zero-tolerance policy for that type of shit. That was why I paid the big bucks to stay there.

I pulled into the alleyway and shot Ashley a message. I was sitting right by the door, waiting for her to emerge. I saw the doorknob jiggle before the door flew open, and a smile graced my cheeks. In a fit of red hair with her glasses slung on her face, Ashley opened my car door and sank into the seat.

"Whisk me away, driver."

"My pleasure," I said.

I backed us down the alleyway and kept to all the back roads. It tacked thirty minutes onto our trip, but it helped me make sure no one was following us. We hit a barren stretch of the road that ran parallel to the ocean, and I rolled Ashley's window down.

Her eyes closed as she took in the salted air, and I could see her visibly relax.

I took a chance and reached over to take her hand. Her eyes popped open, and I waited for her to pull away. Her eyes dipped into her lap, watching my fingers curl over her skin.

Instead of pulling away, she sat back and closed her eyes.

She was still comfortable with me. Even after everything that had transpired, she was still comfortable. A spark of hope ignited in my toes as a smile pulled across my cheeks. If I could show her I was still the man she knew I was, then things might be fixable with us, which was all I really wanted. For things to be okay between us.

I pulled in front of my private beach house, and there wasn't another person in sight. The nearest bungalows were a mile in either direction, and the only thing I could hear were the crashing of the waves. Ashley lifted her head and looked around, her eyes growing wide when she saw how remote it really was out here.

"Hungry?" I asked.

"Starving," she said.

We took our bags up the steps before I let her in. It was a small space, but it had a great deal of privacy. There was a loft with windows that overlooked the ocean, and on the main floor was the kitchen, the decadent bathroom, and the living room that backed up to a sliding glass door. The porch had a set of steps jutting right into the sand, leading straight out to the ocean and all it had to offer.

"It's a beautiful view out here," Ashley said.

"It's better with you in it," I said. "How does grilled chicken and vegetables sound?"

I whipped us up some food in the kitchen as Ashley nursed a glass of wine. She was out on the porch, her feet kicked up on the railing as she sat back in one of my chairs. Barbecue grilled chicken with garlic and lemon vegetables was on the menu for an early dinner, and there were plenty of leftovers if we got hungry later.

"Whatever it is, it smells wonderful," Ashley said.

"Already forget what I was cooking?"

"Zoning out. I haven't done that in so long."

"Then zone out all you want. That's what this trip is for," I said.

I poured myself a glass of wine, and the two of us ate in silence, but the silence wasn't uncomfortable this time. It was usual. Warming. Reminiscent of how things were between us. I scooted my foot underneath the table and rested it against hers, and her head flew up to catch my eyes. There was still a touch of hesitancy there. I could see her debating whether this was a good idea.

But she didn't draw back, and I didn't pull away.

I picked up our plates when we were both finished and dumped them into the sink. I wanted to take Ashley on a walk along the beach. That was one of the last activities we had enjoyed together before everything went to shit, and I wanted her to know we could still have those moments. Those pocketed moments where the only thing that mattered was the two of us.

"We did this when I first moved into my apartment," Ashley said.

"It's one of my favorite memories of us."

"We talk about it like it was years ago."

"It feels like it sometimes."

"I can't believe you have this beach all to yourself. I'd never come home if I owned a place like this."

"There are times when I come out here and work from that porch. It's never more than a couple of days at a time, but it's really a nice getaway."

"A couple of days? I'd never come home if it was up to me."

"You really like it that much out here?" I asked.

"I love it. The view. The privacy. The quiet. I can't remember the last time life was this quiet."

I squeezed her hand, allowing our fingers to lace together as the waves lapped against our ankles.

"How's your mother doing?" I asked.

"Not good," Ashley said with a sigh. "But I'm coming to terms with it."

"What's going on?"

"Oh, you know. She's not lucid very often. She's combative. She's hitting the nurses now."

"What?" I asked.

"Yeah. It's common when Alzheimer's degenerates like that. The person gets to a point where their unfamiliarity with things makes them angry because they're aware of the fact they can't remember but don't know why."

"I can't even imagine."

"Once someone becomes physically combative, it's only a matter of time. The mood swings and the frustration mean the preventative medication is no longer working. It means she's beyond help at this point."

"I'm so sorry, Ashley."

"Don't worry about it. I mean, it's not your problem to worry over."

"I feel it is."

"Why?" she asked.

"Because I care about you."

Our walking ceased, and Ashley craned her neck to up see me. Her eyes danced between mine as the ocean drenched up the backs of our calves. I lifted my hand to her face and smoothed her hair back, tucking it behind her ear.

I watched her nuzzle into my palm as my hand rested against her cheek.

"Come on. I want to show you my favorite spot on this stretch," I said.

I took the lead as Ashley followed behind me. Our hands were still connected as we walked along the shoreline. Little by little, I felt like things were smoothing over between us. Little by little, I was seeing the Ashley I once had shining through the cracks of the facade she was trying to put up. It was in the small things. The way she nuzzled still into my touch or the way she told me to kiss her. The way her pupils still dilated when she looked at me and the way her hand seemed to tighten in mine whenever she thought I was going to pull away.

I came upon the rocks that surrounded the little, abandoned hut, tucked away from the rest of the world.

"What is that?" Ashley asked.

"Come on. Let me show you."

I walked us up to it and ducked into the hut. There was nothing special about it. It was surrounded by rocks and had this little, thatched roof. It was open only on one side, and that was the side that faced the ocean. There were a couple of lounge chairs I had stored in here for whenever I wanted to come and take a nap.

"Here. Take a seat," I said.

I helped Ashley into her lounger before I sat down in mine. The sounds of the ocean echoed off the small curved walls as the wind ruffled the roof. Ashley's smile was broad as she leaned back in the chair with a perfect view of the ocean, our presence completely closed off from everywhere else. And it was quiet, something Ashley needed right now.

"I could go to sleep in something like this," she said.

"Then do it," I said.

"What?"

I looked over at her and smoothed my hand along her leg.

"If you want to take a nap, then take a nap. I do it every time I come in here."

"So this is yours?" she asked.

"In a way. I'm not sure who made it, but whoever it was, they abandoned it. I put a floor in it so sand wouldn't get everywhere and stacked a few rocks to cover up the windows on the sides, but yeah. It's essentially mine."

"Does anyone ever find it and use it?" she asked.

"Nope. No one's allowed to come this far onto my beach, remember?" I asked.

"Your beach," she said with a giggle.

"Yes, my beach."

Her hand rested over mine, but she didn't pick it up off her leg. She wrapped her fingers around mine and leaned back, a small sigh escaping her lips. I watched her eyes fluttered closed, and I sat there, reveling in her beauty while the wind whipped against the hut.

She looked beautiful when she was sleeping. And I decided a nice nap might do me a bit of good, too.

Chapter 14

Ashley

I woke up with Jimmy's hand still secured in my own. The sun was beginning to set, and the ocean sounded closer than ever before. I fluttered my eyes open and saw Jimmy sleeping next to me as soft snores fell from his lips.

I felt incredible. Alive. Beautiful.

Our day on the beach had been wonderful. The food he cooked was splendid, and the wine had been a wonderful way to top it all off. The long walk we took was relaxing, and the moment served to remind me of how natural things felt between us and how easy it was to talk with Jimmy about things like my mother. Waking up with the sun shining through the door of this hut thing felt fantastic like I had been bathed in a cleansing water and pulled free of all the stress that had been chaining me down for days.

I could do this over and over again and never want for anything else.

But I was scared to let Jimmy back in. I was scared to give this another shot. The ache in my heart was still there from all the things we had said to one another. I felt Jimmy stirring, and I looked over at him, watching as his eyes peeled open. A sleepy smile crossed his cheeks as he brought my hand to his lips.

His kiss shot electricity up my arm.

"I don't know about you," he said, "but I could use some coffee."

"I'm always up for coffee. What did you have in mind?" I asked.

"There's this small breakfast cafe across the street from where we are. It's run by this wonderful couple. And they make the best coffee."

"Then let's go," I said. "I'm always up for the best coffee in town."

We emerged from the hut hand in hand, and we made our way up the beach. We ran across the road, the wind whipping through my hair. I ran into Jimmy's arms, and he twirled me around, my arms wrapped tightly around his neck.

He settled me down on the sidewalk, and it took me a second to rip my gaze from his.

"Ready for some coffee?" I asked.

"Always when it comes to their coffee."

Jimmy opened the door for me and he was right. The place was charming. There were mismatched tables and chairs everywhere as well as a few plush couches over in the corner. There was an older woman behind the counter with beautiful white hair, and an older man with gray hair emerged from the back.

"Jimmy! What a surprise."

"Bernie. It's good to see you again."

I watched the two men embrace before Jimmy turned to me.

"And this lovely woman is Ashley," he said.

"It's wonderful to meet you, Ashley," Bernie said.

"The pleasure's all mine," I said.

"This beautiful woman is my lovely wife, Patrice. Been married for fifty-one years, her and I," Bernie said.

"Fifty-one years?" I asked. "But you can't be any older than—"

"I know, I know. We were married young," Patrice said. "Nineteen to be exact."

"I hear you guys have the best cup of coffee in town," I said.

"Did Jimmy tell you that? He better have told you that," Bernie said.

"He definitely told me that," I said with a giggle.

"Good. Two cups of coffee?" Patrice asked.

"And two of those mozzarella and buffalo chicken sandwiches you guys make," Jimmy said. "Trust me, Ashley. They're out of this world."

"Ranch for both?" Bernie asked.

"Please," I said.

"So Ashley. How did you hook up with a guy like Jimmy?" Patrice asked.

I looked over at him warily, and he nodded his head.

Like it was okay during all this turmoil to tell them how we really met.

"Um, well, we met at a party," I said.

"One of Jimmy's work shindigs?" Bernie asked.

"It's okay," Jimmy said. "They're the only two I trust."

"Yes, at one of his work parties," I said.

"Let me guess. One-night stand and the rest was history?" Patrice asked.

I choked on my own spit as she handed two cups of coffee to Jimmy.

"Um."

"It's okay, sweetheart. That's actually similar to how Bernie and I met," she said.

"How did you two meet?" I asked.

"At a birthday party, of all places. Her sister was celebrating her twenty-first, and I was invited," Bernie said.

"His brother is married to my older sister," Patrice said.

"Oh, wow. That's rare," I said.

"That's one way to put it. We danced the night away, and he kissed me, and the rest was history. We were married less than a year later despite our parents' protests, and here we are," she said.

"Seven kids and four grandkids later," Bernie said.

"Seven children?" I asked.

"We're leaving this place to the eldest. He loves it here. He'll take over our beach house when we pass, and he'll be running this place like it needs to be," Patrice said.

"Then hopefully one of our grandkids will take it over. He's got two little girls that we hope will grow up with a love for this place like he's got," Bernie said.

I took a sip of the coffee Jimmy handed me, and I moaned.

"Oh my gosh," I said.

"I'm telling you. I don't know what they do to it," Jimmy said.

"Two buffalo mozzarella sandwiches with ranch," Bernie said.

"That thing is massive," I said.

"We've got to-go boxes. Don't worry," Patrice said.

I took my plate from Bernie and followed Jimmy to a table in the corner. The sandwich already had my mouth watering, and the coffee was to die for. I would definitely be getting another cup before we left to go back to the world of stress and lies in order to save our asses.

"Ashley?"

"Mhm?"

"I'm sorry."

I took a sip of my coffee as my eyes connected with his.

"I know you are," I said. "And I am too."

"I handled the stress of everything happening poorly, and you're right. I should have listened to you from the very beginning. I had no reason to doubt you, and I called you some ugly things I don't know if I'll ever be able to take back."

"I wasn't in the best form either. I accused you of not caring about your company, and I know that's not true."

"I want a second chance at us, Ashley."

I closed my eyes and drew in a deep breath.

"I want to try and make this work."

"You just told the press we weren't together, Jimmy. Ever," I said.

"When your reputation was on the line, I was willing to say anything. I still am. Because there's no reason for them to attack you in the media. None whatsoever. And so long as I can protect your reputation,

I'll say whatever it takes, but that doesn't mean I don't want to be with you. It means we would have to be careful."

"I'm scared, Jimmy. If someone finds out—"

"Then we'll deal with it together. As a team. I will always provide a wall between you and the press. You will never have to fight that battle alone, nor will you ever have to face it head-on."

"I'm not worried about that. I mean, I am. But ..."

"What is it?" he asked. "What are you worried about?"

"I'm worried you'll hurt me again, and it'll only prove I'm right."

I felt a tear slide down my face as Jimmy cupped my cheek.

"And I don't want to be right about that," I said.

"You won't be. So long as I'm breathing, I won't hurt you again, and I will always trust your opinion, especially after something like this. If you want to take it slow, that's fine. I'll do it. I just want you, Ashley, no matter what I have to do to get there."

"Slow might be a good thing. We took things pretty fast the first time around. Slow might do us some good."

"Then slow it is," he said.

We finished our sandwiches and grabbed another cup of coffee before heading out. We walked hand in hand down the sidewalk, making our way slowly back to his beach house. Things felt... okay. Not grand. Not splendid. But okay. Simple. Fluid. I felt the stress melting from my body with every step I took toward Jimmy's place.

We would be okay.

Somewhere in the pit of my gut, I knew we would be okay if we took it slow.

We got back to Jimmy's place, but we didn't go inside. Instead, we sat on the porch and finished off our coffees. The sun was quickly setting below the ocean, blanketing our area in a nighttime hue.

And there was a look in Jimmy's eyes I couldn't deny.

I stood up from my chair and straddled his lap. His hands fell to my hips as my dress fluttered around my thighs. Our foreheads connected, and I closed my eyes, my body coming to life as his thumbs stroked my skin.

I could taste the coffee on his lips as our tongues connected.

I could feel him already growing to life, pressing against me as his hands gathered my dress up to my hips. I ran my hand through his hair, clinging to him while he pushed his pants down his legs.

Then I pulled my panties off to the side before he slid in.

There was no pretense and no foreplay. No heavy petting and no hickies. There was only the setting of the sun, the freedom of the moment, and my want for him. His hands ran up and down my thighs as I coated his cock, my arousal slowly pooling for him. Our lips moved together, slowly and desperately as our tongues battled for dominance. I could feel him growing, twitching against my walls as his hands explored my body. Rose up my back. Cupped my clothed breasts. Grabbed my ass and rolled me deeper.

I moaned into his lips as his trimmed curls found my clit. I ground into him as nighttime hung fully in the air. My lower lip trembled, and electricity shot through my body. He felt so good. As good as he did the first time and better than he had last weekend.

He rolled me faster into him, his hips leaving the chair. He thrust into me, trying to keep our movements as controlled as possible. The waves were washing ashore, and the stars were twinkling above. There wasn't a sound from the city we could hear. The only thing that graced my eardrums was the panting of Jimmy's breath as his lips cascaded down my neck.

"Jimmy," I said breathlessly. "I'm almost there."

My legs began to quiver, and my toes began to curl. My face fell into the crook of his neck as he continued to kiss my skin. His fingertips dug into my ass, and his movements began to stutter. I rocked against him, my pussy sucking him deeper as it began to flutter around his cock.

"I can feel you. I can feel you. I can feel you."

He chanted it like a prayer. Like the greatest relief he had ever experienced. His entire body shook as I clung to him, my arms wrapped tightly around his neck.

His long, strong arms gripped me tightly into him, pressing my curves into his strength. Then, with a groan, he pumped me full of his come.

I sighed into the crook of his neck as tears of happiness lined my eyes. I had missed this man. For all the shit we had been through, I had missed every inch of him.

We sat there, my body cradled into his. His cock began to soften as our juices ran down onto the seat. He picked me up to take me inside, but his pants fell down around his legs, and he shuffled us into the beach house. I giggled into his neck, feeling him reach out as he slid the glass door closed.

"Where are we going?" I asked.

"To bed. I want to hold you while we look out over the ocean."

Then he stepped out of his pants, carried me up the stairs, and laid me down in his bed. His body fell against mine as his hand stroked my legs, and his lips kissed my skin. He sent shivers up and down my spine while we gazed out along the water, the stress of work slowly falling to the back of my mind.

I could get used to something like this. All we had to do was keep our heads above water long enough.

Chapter 15

Jimmy

I woke up with Ashley in my arms, and I was reluctant to let her go. But I knew we had to be getting back. With all the issues surrounding the company, I couldn't afford to be gone an entire weekend, which I hated because it was what Ashley deserved. I watched her sleep until she stirred in my arms. The ocean sun suited her well. When all of this was over and we could go public with our relationship, I vowed to bring her back here every single weekend. Maybe if her mother was doing well, we could bring her too. I was sure she would love a walk in the sand, no matter her lucidity.

At least, I hoped that was something I could do for Ashley.

The two of us stopped in for coffee and a danish before we got on the road. I wanted to make sure the heat was completely off us. My plan was to take us to my place first and hang out for a little bit, and then I would take her back to her apartment. My place was closer than hers, and we could bypass the afternoon rush of people in the street easier that way.

Ashley seemed okay with the plan, so I stuck to the back roads to get back to my apartment.

The elevator doors opened, and I ushered her out into the hallway. We turned to get to my front door, but Ashley stopped in her tracks. I ran right into her, almost knocking her to the ground. I caught her in my arms and steadied her on her feet, but her eyes were locked in front of her.

"Ashley, what's—?"

I looked up to see one of the FBI guys standing at my front door. He was leaning against the wall, like he'd been waiting for me. There was shock on his face at seeing the two of us together in such relaxed attire with coffees in our hands. He'd seen me throw my arms around Ashley, and I could tell she was panicking.

"Mr. Sheldon."

"Agent. With all due respect, what are you doing standing at my door?" I asked.

"I was waiting for you. I didn't know you would have company."

"Could you not have called?" I asked.

"I did, but you weren't picking up."

"Because I was out of town."

"So I came to your front door to wait. You said you were coming back in this afternoon. Figured the information I had was worth it."

"What information?" I asked.

"I thought the two of you weren't a thing?" he asked.

I looked down at Ashley who had panic written all over her forehead. So I stepped in front of her to rip the agent's eyes from her to me.

"Why are you together if you're not a thing?" the agent asked.

"Not that it's any of your business in the first place, but—"

"He was trying to protect his reputation," Ashley said.

She stepped out from behind me and linked her arm with mine.

"And hers," I said. "Neither of us are ready to go public, especially with everything that's happening with the company. And I would appreciate it if you understood and respected our wishes."

"Uh-huh," the agent said. "I had a feeling."

"What do you mean?" Ashley asked.

"The way you two have been actively avoiding one another since her return," he said. "It screams 'couple trying to hide it.'"

"No, it doesn't," I said.

"It really does," the agent said.

"We would like it if you respected our privacy enough to keep it under wraps," Ashley said.

"Don't worry. The FBI isn't interested in office romances, but we are interested in Markus.

"What's happened?" I asked.

"Because Markus made bail, the first thing he did was fly back to Canada. Only he's not there any longer," the agent said.

"What the hell does that mean?" I asked.

"Markus has fled Canada because the fraud goes deeper than we thought. We stumbled on it last night. With a trail of proof we uncovered, we have reason to believe Mr. Bryant was running a scam in his own company."

I felt Ashley nudge me as I bit down on my tongue.

"Tell him," Ashley said.

"Tell him what?" the agent asked.

I looked down at Ashley, and she gazed up at me. I had to draw from her well of strength because I couldn't do this on my own. I was about to sell the only man I had ever truly respected up the river, and it made me sick. He'd been a man I'd trusted with my own success, my own life, my memories and my past and everything else I had to offer.

A man I had come to love was nothing more than a Bernie Madoff mimic.

"You're going to be upset, so hear me out," I said.

"Try me," the agent said.

"I had my COO, Ross Fowler, retain one of the private investigators we used to originally dig into Markus."

"Great," the agent said.

"We found that he was forging my signature on documents to invest in companies he's also been robbing. Ace-Landic and Harold & Lace, to be exact."

"And when were you going to step forward with this?"

"Now," I said.

"Why the hell didn't you do it sooner?"

"Because Markus was like a father to Jimmy, and he needed time to emotionally digest what was going on," Ashley said.

I looked down at her and saw a protective fire in her eye.

"You know what this looks like? Collusion," the agent said.

"Well, it's not," Ashley said. "It's a man coming to terms with his own conscience before he sells the only man he ever considered a father up the damn river. And if you attempt to stick anything else onto this, I've got no issues dragging you through the mud."

I was shocked at Ashley's outburst, but my heart swelled with pride. No woman would come to blows with an FBI agent like that if she didn't still care like I did.

"I want that evidence handed over today," the agent said. "If he's using your signature and we can prove you had no hand in those investments, we've got him nailed. That's the missing link."

Ashley nudged me again, and it caused me to snicker.

"I'll have Ross call the PI and have everything delivered within the hour," I said.

"Good. And from now on? Leave the investigating to us."

"No problem," I said with a grin.

I watched the agent walk down the hallway as I pulled my phone out of my pocket. I unlocked the door and ushered Ashley in while I called Ross. I told him what was going on and that he needed to get in contact with the PI. That information needed to be handed over to the FBI as well as my lawyer. I hung up the phone and tossed it onto the couch, my anger trying to get the best of me again.

How the hell had Markus turned out to be such a scumbag? How many other companies had he done this to? How many people was he siphoning money off of because of me?

How many other companies like mine had he scammed?

"Jimmy?"

I felt Ashley's hand fall on my shoulder as I sat onto the couch.

"Jimmy, talk to me."

"Is it possible Markus is the next Bernie Madoff?" I asked.

"Depends if he was running a Ponzi scheme," she said.

"How in the world could I have been so blind?"

"Jimmy, men like Markus literally do this for a living. This is how he's been living his life, surviving and thriving. Conning is his life's work."

"His own company, Ashley. All those people will be out of jobs, many arrested for things they didn't even know they were doing. What if he's set up one of them to take the fall while he runs to a country with no extradition?"

"Wow, this has been on your mind, hasn't it?" she asked.

"I can't put anything past him now. A man I thought was tried-and-true and faithful to his core is slowly turning out to be a mastermind criminal. He's got a contingency plan somewhere. What if this is it?" I asked.

"You can't concern yourself with that. You have a company that needs you, that needs your strength."

"I don't feel very strong right now. I feel like every time I turn around, another rug I step on is ripped from underneath me. Fleeing Canada? Where the hell did the man go?"

"I'm sure they're trying to figure that out," she said.

"I'm sorry. I know this is the last thing you wanted to walk into after our night at the beach."

"True, but I haven't left. We still have the afternoon. Why don't I take you up on that movie?"

I looked over at her, watching as the sun illuminated her body.

"Dinner and a movie?" I asked.

"Dinner and a movie sounds fabulous," she said.

Chapter 16

Ashley

I walked into work with everyone's eyes on me. They were openly gawking at me and pointing their fingers. A few women were looking down their noses at me as I walked through the lobby. What in the world was going on? I took the elevator up to the top floor and made my way to my office, but once I got there I saw what was going on.

I ripped the picture off my door and stared at it.

It was the front of one of the tabloid magazines. The words 'Liar, Liar, Pants On Fire' was strewn across the front. Then there, in the middle of the page, was a picture of Jimmy and me holding hands on the beach. It was a close-up, digital photograph of the highest quality.

Tears sprang to my eyes as I slammed myself into my office. I couldn't believe it. Someone had perched on the side of the fucking beach and stalked us while we were trying to take some time for ourselves. I slammed the door behind me and pressed myself against it, shielding everyone from my tears. I was tired of holding them back.

I slid to my knees as I clutched the picture to my chest. A wonderful set of moments between Jimmy and me, obliterated because some money-hungry paparazzi wanted a picture of us that desperately. Tears dripped onto my thighs as I leaned heavily on the door.

I felt weaker than I ever had in my life.

Was being with Jimmy worth it? Was this the life we were going to lead from now on? Was I going to lose my job over this? Surely the board would call for it. They would tell Jimmy to get rid of me, and he would have to in order to save his company, in order to do the one thing I accused him of not doing because he was too focused on me.

Shit.

If it wasn't one thing, it was another. I turned around and pressed my back to the door, pulling my knees to my chest. There was always something trying to hurt our image or Jimmy's image or the company's image. So what if we were together? Who cared? This company was roaring with success, and we provided outstanding luxury services to a plethora of clients.

Who cared who was screwing who?

I wasn't sure if I could do this. I knew if I picked up my phone, the tabloids and the media would be ripping me to shreds. Not Jimmy, because he was a man. A virile billionaire who could lay his seed wherever he wanted. But the homely, quiet accountant? I'd be a whore. A bitch. A money-hungry boss fucker who sucked her way to the top. He would be praised, and I would be ostracized, and people would jeer at me on the street like they were in the office this morning.

It was out in the open because someone wanted to profit off our picture.

I reached up to lock my door and put all my calls on hold. I sat at my desk, my tears dripping onto the picture. I didn't know what to do. I knew we couldn't continue like this, but I'd walked away from the past weekend with so much hope. I thought things were okay and that we were going to be able to get running in the right direction. Not even twenty-four hours later, I was slapped with the reality that we might not be okay. I might not be able to be with the man I still loved.

I saw my phone lighting up even though it wasn't ringing in the office. I tossed the front page of the magazine onto my desk and decided to ignore the call. I didn't want to pick it up and talk to whoever was on the other end. It was probably some reporter trying to hound me for a quote or ask me what it was like to suck my boss's cock for money. I didn't want to deal with it.

Until I saw it light up again.

I peeked out my window and glanced over at Jimmy's office. His door was open. He had his phone to his ear, and he was staring at my door. I reached for the phone and picked it up, holding it to my ear as I tried to gather myself.

But the second I drew in a deep breath, he knew what was going on.

"Please don't cry," he said.

"What would you rather me do? Burn down the building?" I asked.

"Don't do that, either. That would be a mess I couldn't clean up."

"That makes me think you still feel like you can clean this one up."

"I'm working on it," he said. "Are you okay?"

"No. No, Jimmy. I'm not okay. I haven't taken a look at any of the other magazines, but I'm sure they're doing what they did before, ripping us to shreds and calling me some version of an office whore."

"That's one way to put it," he said.

"Are you trying to make me feel better?"

"No. I'm trying to talk to you on how we can make this better."

"Maybe we can't, Jimmy."

His eyes found mine through the small part of the unfrosted glass sitting next to my door.

"What do you mean?" he asked.

"Maybe this can't happen between us."

"You don't mean that."

"I wish I didn't, but what if it's true?" I asked. "What if we really can't be together because they'll slaughter us every time we are?"

"The only reason they're doing this is because of the scandal going on with my company."

"And why did they do it the first time? Because I'm pretty sure they found out about it so you could try and dig me out of that issue the first time around."

"Honestly, I don't know, but losing you isn't an option, Ashley. Not again."

"Do we get options with something like this?" I asked.

"I'll create them. That's what I've always done in my life, created options I could choose from."

"You said that was a private beach where no one would find us because they weren't allowed. And now, we've been outed."

"So let's stay out," he said.

"What?" I asked.

"Let's stay out. Maybe we should have said we did have something going on. Every single article is now reaming me on lying to the press. What if we had come clean in the first place?"

"We can't turn back time, Jimmy."

"But we can admit it now."

"Jimmy, we just got our feet back on solid ground. We're taking things slowly, remember?" I asked.

"All I know is I want to be with you, and if going to the press and telling them we're together gives me that, then I'm willing to do it."

"Then what about me? What about what I want?"

"I'm asking you now. What is it you want?"

My eyes gazed into my lap as I played with the cord of the phone. My mind was spinning at a thousand miles a second, and I could see someone standing outside my office. I tensed up in my chair and prepared myself for a fight, but Jimmy's voice settled me down.

"It's only Ross. He's waiting for us to finish up so he can give you something."

"What is it?" I asked.

"Balance sheets."

"That my responsibility now?"

"Until we can prove to the investors no other mysterious transactions are being made, yes," he said.

"Tell Ross to slip them under my door."

I watched the file folder appear from underneath the doorway before he walked away. I watched his body through the small sliver of unfrosted glass as I sank back into my seat. Life went on. That was the lesson surrounding all of this. Life went on, and if I allowed the circumstances of my life to control my actions, then I would never be happy. I would always be chasing after the next space of relief instead of an everlasting happiness.

But Jimmy's company couldn't tank over this. I was going to make sure that didn't happen.

"I'm sorry for all this," Jimmy said. "I should've kept an eye out on the corners of the road."

"This isn't your fault. It's a series of very unfortunate events that have careened way out of control," I said.

"I'll hold a press conference later and try to drain the heat off you again."

"I don't think that's smart. If you lied in one press conference, they'll be prepared for you to lie in another one. They'll dissect your every word for weeks to come."

"But they won't be talking about it."

"Which does no one any good if this company goes under for it. Look, when the time is right, we'll tell people. Okay? But for now, we need to wait until the heat from this fraud wears off. If anything, hold a press conference about that, but there's too much going on right now to focus on the immediate threat. Play the game a few steps ahead, Jimmy. It's the only thing that's going to save your company."

I looked back up at him through the glass, and I sighed. I held the silent phone to my ear as Jimmy's gaze held mine. His beautiful blue eyes and his stoic face. I was in love with that face. And the man attached to that face.

"I know you're right," Jimmy said.

"So no press conference?"

"Does this mean you're staying with me? At least a little while longer?" he asked.

"Yes," I said. "It does."

"Then no press conference. I'll wait until the heat dies down off this fraud issue with Markus, and then we'll go from there."

"And in the meantime, if we want time together, we'll keep it under wraps. We won't flaunt it, but we won't intentionally try to hide it."

"I can do that," he said.

"Take a deep breath, Jimmy. We're going to get through this."

"I never thought I'd hear you say those words to me again."

I could hear the sadness in his voice, sadness laced with regret. I closed my eyes and felt my jaw quivering, but I wasn't going to lose it over the phone. I wasn't going to cry in this office full of idiots.

"I'll talk with you soon, okay?" I asked.

"Have a good day, Ashley," he said.

I worked through my day as best as I could, and then I made my way home. I didn't stop by Jimmy's office or try to go out of my way to see how he was doing. People's eyes were all over me, and everywhere I turned, someone was taping another front-page article of me to my door. Of course, they weren't doing it to Jimmy, but me? Oh, yeah. But I ripped every single one of them down and made sure everyone saw me throwing it in the trash can.

I walked into my apartment with Cass sitting on my couch. She had a piping hot pizza sitting on the coffee table, and Chipper was in her arms. She turned around as my purse dropped to the floor, and I stumbled into her arms as she shot up to catch me.

"I don't know what to do," I said as I cried into her. "I don't know what to do anymore."

"I wish I could tell you," Cass said. "I wish I had all the answers to your problems right now."

"They're slaughtering us."

"I know."

"It's everywhere."

"I know."

"I love him, Cass. He's hurting, and I love him, and I can't do anything about his pain."

She clutched me in her arms as Chipper ran around our feet. We sat down on the couch, the smell of pizza filling my apartment. Chipper climbed onto my lap and nestled into me, trying to provide me with some sort of comfort.

"You really love him?" she asked.

"I really do," I said with a sniffle.

"Then you have to stand by him. No matter what comes or what's thrown your way, the two of you have to get through this together."

"I have no idea how to deal with something like this," I said.

"Neither do I, but I know you. I know at least one time today, you've questioned whether or not to walk away from him. If you love Jimmy, don't."

I pulled away from my best friend as her hands cupped my cheeks. Her thumbs wiped at my tears as Chipper nuzzled underneath my hand. I sighed and closed my eyes, allowing my nostrils to fill with the sweet scent of dinner.

"Now, we're going to sit here with this lemonade I made and this pizza I ordered, and you're going to tell me all about this secret weekend," Cass said.

"I don't know if I—"

"Just the good stuff. None of the bad. Something happened with you two this weekend because you're openly admitting how you feel about him. That's huge. And I want to know what happened. But not only that, you need to remind yourself that this was a good weekend. Despite what you walked back into this morning, it was a good weekend. You can't let someone take that from you. You have to be stronger than that."

"I'm tired of being strong, Cass. I'm strong for Mom, and I was strong for the investors. Now, I have to be strong for Jimmy. Who's going to be strong for me?"

"I am," she said. "Then when Jimmy pulls himself together, he will be. He's allowed to break down and lean on you, so long as he does the same when it's your turn."

"We had a fabulous weekend," I said breathlessly.

"Then take this slice of pizza, and tell me how it went."

Chapter 17

Jimmy

"So, thanks for telling the FBI before you told me," Trish said.

"What can I say? They cornered me at my home," I said.

"Don't worry about it. What's done is done. I got that snarky as hell FBI agent transferred off this case. He was really pushing the idea that you were intentionally covering this up."

"Well, thanks for that," I said.

"However, his idea has tainted some other officers on the case, which makes this trickier than usual."

"Of fucking course, it does."

That seemed to be the motto for every damn day of my life.

"The plea bargain has been thrown out the window with all of this new information, which means this will go to trial, but trial for things like this is a long, drawn-out process."

"I know, but he needs to pay for what he's done to my company and to others."

"The FBI is starting to branch out. With proof he forged your signature and was investing on behalf of your company without your knowledge, who knows how many pies this man had his hands in? They're digging into every possible avenue, but the digging itself could take months."

"Great," I said. "Just what I need."

"With men like him, there are always more. But here are the important points. Right now, Markus has fled Canada. Right now, there's no reason to suggest he's left the continent. The assets in his name are frozen, and the assets in his girlfriend's name have been drained. The FBI are looking into assets he might've put in his mother's name as well as his previous wife's name, but they aren't coming up with anything."

"Which means?"

"There's a good chance he's still in the States."

"I thought he went back to Canada, though."

"That FBI agent didn't tell you much, did he?" she asked.

"Nope. He was too focused on the fact that I was with Ashley."

"Well, that's a nice bomb to drop on me. Thanks. I would've been focused on that too."

"Get over it. We deserve to be happy."

"Not arguing that point. How do you keep screwing things up? Anyway, back on topic. Markus went back to Canada until he figured out the federal authorities there were cooperating with us, which meant he had as much of a chance to end up in prison here as he did in Canada. So he fell off the face of the map."

"Wait, he disappeared?" I asked.

"The FBI have him traveling in a stolen rental car back over the border into the US, but no one has picked him up on any cameras in any of the airports."

"I can't keep up with all this shit. Are they going to get him back into custody or not?" I asked.

"I'll keep you updated on that as it happens. That's where they are right now. Given that other companies are starting an uproar over all of this, I'm sure it won't be long before someone somewhere turns him over. Madoff couldn't hide from this, and neither can Markus."

"What do you need from me?" I asked.

"Exact numbers. I need Ross and Ashley to get me and the FBI exact numbers to the penny of what he took. No rounding off, no splitting hairs. From as far back in Big Steps and all your sub-companies as you can go. The more clear-cut proof we have that doesn't require the jury to wade through calculations and scribbles, the better off we are in court."

"Done," I said.

"I'm serious. Not having those numbers in a clear, concise format with easy-to-read proof could get this entire thing thrown out, Jimmy."

"Ashley and Ross will be on it. I promise. I'm not letting this asshole walk," I said. "I'll keep in touch."

My lawyer got up and walked out of the room, but I wasn't alone for long. Soon, the investors started piling in, every single fucking one of them. I furrowed my brow as they all sat down around me, taking up the space at the table they'd just been at a few days prior.

"Is there a meeting I'm forgetting about?" I asked.

"We need to talk, Sheldon."

"About what?" I asked.

"About where our money's going and what's happening with this investigation."

"Miss Ternbeau is working on your monthly PDF documents this week. You'll have them in your inbox the same time as you always do," I said.

Then, Mr. Matthews slid one of the tabloid papers across the table at me.

"Care to explain this?" he asked.

"That would be me and Ashley holding hands on a beach," I said.

"You told the media the two of you weren't together," he said.

"In order to spare her reputation, yes."

"You lied to the media. When were you going to come clean to us that our personal accountant was your mistress?"

"First off, she's not a mistress. She's my girlfriend. Secondly, I was going to wait until the head of this fraud died down before Ashley and I went public with our relationship."

"So you are with her."

"Yes, I am," I said.

"Jimmy, this doesn't look good, and you know it," an investor said.

"This is going to hit you where it hurts the most," another said.

"We're tackling one issue at a time," I said.

"And speaking of those issues, why can't we get updates on the investigation? It's our money that's being stolen."

"Correction, it was your money that was being stolen. Nothing is being stolen now, "I said.

"You have no proof of that."

"Because next month's balance sheets haven't happened yet because it's not next month."

"Don't get snarky with me, Sheldon."

"Then listen to what I have to say, Mr. Matthews. I'm not sure how you became the spokesperson for every single investor on this board, but I don't like it. Your checks don't clear, and you talk down to Miss Ternbeau every single chance you get. Putting both of those issues aside, I can't prove to you this company is okay until the end of next month. You want clear balance sheets, but they won't happen until the end of next month. Why? Because Markus was an investor on this board until a week ago, which means two weeks' worth of withdrawals will still be on this month's balance sheets. Are you still with me?" I asked.

Mr. Matthews drew in a deep breath as the investors cleared their throats.

"We're worried about our money," he said. "I think it's okay to speak for everyone when I say that."

"Have you checked your bank accounts recently? Because I'm pretty sure profits still dropped in there this morning," I said.

"Yes, and twenty million dollars of our own money has been funneling out this door for over a decade," an investor said.

"Look, there's nothing I can do about that. Eventually, we will see that money back. Everything Mr. Bryant owns will be liquidated and distributed among the companies he stole from."

"So there's more?" Matthews asked.

"Yes, there's more. Two of my subcompanies and at least two more outside companies in Miami. He was also defrauding his own company. A regular Bernie Madoff he was."

"Does the FBI know this?"

"They do. They're digging into every single branch-off he could've made to steal from other companies. You guys seem to come at me like this doesn't affect me, when really I've got twenty men up in arms about things that don't affect them. And before you bite into me for that statement, let me remind you that you did see profit today. And nothing about that profit dropped. You still saw the same return Miss Ternbeau predicted for you, and you will continue to see the same profit despite what happens because I'm holding this fort down, and I'm pushing this company forward, and I'm getting it through its most brutal time."

"And we appreciate that," Matthews said, "but your reputation with the media is being decimated. Have you not turned on a television?"

"I've been staying away from the media since they want to chew me up and spit me out," I said.

"How could we not have seen this sooner?" an investor asked.

"Because the accountant before Ashley did a shit job. Which was why I hired Ashley in the first place."

"Ashley?" Matthews asked.

"Do you have a problem with her having a first name?" I asked.

"Don't get snarky with us. We feed this company," an investor said.

"Right now, all you're doing is weighing this company down more. I could be repairing my image right now, but instead, I'm playing Mommy Dearest to a bunch of men who can't stay out of this building for more than a few days without freaking out."

"Then give us regular updates," Matthews said.

"Stay away long enough for them and you will," I said. "Look, I had no idea that beach trip was going to blow up like it did. But it has, despite the fact that the picture on the front of this garbage newspaper was taken illegally."

"Then I'll end our pointless meeting with this," he said. "Either you clean up your reputation by the end of next month when the clean balance sheets come out, or we'll have to consider pulling out."

"You mean you'll have to consider pulling out?" I asked.

"No, we'll all consider it," another investor said.

I saw all of them nodding their heads, and I felt myself pale. Again? They were threatening my fucking company again? I watched as my investors got up from the table in a huff like the divas they were and marched out of the room.

Leaving me there to reel in the demands they were making once again.

My gut reaction was to talk to Ashley. She always knew how to calm my head during moments like this. But with all eyes on me, it was a bad decision to go traipsing into her office or worse, pull her into mine. I leaned back in my chair and turned it toward the window, staring out over the expanse of Miami. A city that had once held me close in its grasp now had me bleeding in its claws, and I didn't know how to stop it.

For the first time since this entire shitstorm began, my mind was silent. Almost like I'd accepted my own death.

Chapter 18

Ashley

I had to admit, when Jimmy called me and told me to meet him at a hotel, I got a little excited. There was something thrilling about sneaking around with him, something about the forbidden that made everything we were doing more tantalizing. He shot me the number of the hotel room and told me what time to be there, and I went home from work and put on my best outfit, a little black dress with a slit up the back and some black pumps I had bought a couple of weeks back. I put on my best pearls and lined my eyes so they would look bigger than usual. Then I put in my contacts.

I piled my hair on my head, secured it with a pair of chopsticks like I had the night we met, and started for the hotel.

I kept my sunglasses on and stuck to the sides of the place. I walked in through a side door and made my way up to the room. I looked from side to side before I knocked on the door. Then, I raised my arm up and perched my body against the doorframe.

But when Jimmy opened the door, he looked like hell.

"Jimmy, what's wrong?" I asked.

His eyes raked up and down my form before he groaned.

"I'm so sorry," he said.

"What?" I asked. "What's going on?"

I stepped into the room and quickly closed the door behind me.

"You obviously thought–"

"Screw what I thought. Jimmy, you look terrible. What's wrong?" I asked.

"You look amazing. Like you always do."

"Stop changing the subject."

"The investors cornered me today."

"What do you mean cornered? And why wasn't I there?" I asked.

"It happened so quickly. It was right after my meeting with my lawyer."

"How did that go?" I asked.

"As well as could be expected. The digging could take months, and the trial could take months, and everything could take months even though I don't have months."

"What did the investors do?" I asked.

I sat down next to him on the hotel bed and rubbed his back with my hand.

"They're giving me until the end of next month to clean up my act or they're all going to take a step back."

"Why? Did they even check their accounts today?"

"That's exactly what I told them, but their eyes are glued to the media, and apparently, my public image isn't all it's cracked up to be right now. They've once again threatened to pull out if I don't fix things."

"Did you tell them to stick it where the sun doesn't shine?" I asked.

"I was firmer with them than usual. I told them barging in on me like they were doing all the time wasn't helping matters. That I didn't look phased because I had twenty men panicking on me every few hours."

"No, you didn't," I said with a giggle.

"I did. And they weren't appreciative of it."

"Well, they are walking on you a little bit. Are you sure there isn't a chance you could rebuild your investor board?"

"Ashley, it would take years. Big Steps and its subcompanies would go under completely before I rebuilt."

"So what do they want you to do?"

"That's the thing. They didn't give specifics. Just 'clean up your image before the end of next month.'"

"So they don't even have a standard. For all you know, they're planning on pulling out anyway," I said.

"Yep."

"Why didn't you tell me about this at work?"

"Because I figured with all eyes on me it didn't look good pulling you into my office to talk."

"You could've come to mine."

"Still wouldn't have looked good," he said.

"You know, if you wanted to talk about the investors, you could've invited me over to your place," I said.

"Paparazzi are swarming the other side of the road from my complex. They aren't technically breaking the law, but they're being a pain in the ass. I couldn't risk you getting bombarded by them as you came up."

"They aren't at my place."

"Are you saying you don't like the hotel room?" he asked.

"I'm saying I understand. You're floundering, and you're grasping at straws. I'm simply trying to walk through your mindset. What you do understand and what you don't so I can better help you."

"You're amazing, you know that?"

"Only because I have you," I said.

I cupped his face and turned his gaze my way. His back straightened up as his hand perched behind my body. My thumb graced his cheek as his eyes danced between mine, and then his gaze fell to my lips.

"You know, it's kind of hot you wanted me to meet you at a hotel," I said.

"You naughty little girl," Jimmy said with a chuckle.

"Maybe we could make the most of it?"

I watched Jimmy's eyebrows hike up onto his forehead as I leaned in to kiss him. My lips pressed against his, and his hand met my lower back, pulling my body into him. My arms slinked around his neck as we sank to the bed, our tongues colliding in an effortless lust. He rolled me over, my legs parting for him as the fabric of my dress rolled up. His hands were inching up the inside of my thigh as my hands grabbed at the collar of his shirt.

"You're so warm," Jimmy said.

"Touch me," I said. "Anywhere you want."

My hands ran through his hair as his fingers danced along my skin. I loosened his tie and tossed it to the side, my fingers tracing along his buttons. I craved him. My body was shaking for him. I felt his cock growing against my thigh as his hand cupped my clothed pussy.

"So very warm," Jimmy said.

I sighed as he massaged me, his lips pressing into my neck.

I rolled into his hand as I pushed his shirt off his shoulders. His lips drew my skin between his teeth, nibbling little marks onto my skin. I moaned and whimpered, pressing my body into his hand as he teased me with his touch.

But a commotion outside prompted us to stop.

"What is that?" I asked.

"Stay here," Jimmy said.

He got up from the bed, and I sat upright. He held out his hand to get me to stop moving as he moved toward the sliding glass doors. He peered outside as the commotion grew, and I could tell by the fire rising in his eyes that it wasn't good.

"Fuck."

"What is it?" I asked.

"Paparazzi."

"What?" I asked.

"They found us."

"Well, they can't come in, can they?" I asked.

"It doesn't matter. They know we're here together. It'll only be a matter of time before the first article is published."

"How did they figure out we were here?" I asked. "We staggered our entrances. I dressed like I don't normally do. I came in through the side door. I did everything you asked."

"The only thing I can think is someone saw me coming in and alerted the press for a quick fucking buck. Shit."

"What are we going to do?" I asked.

"Give me a second."

But the crowd was growing outside, and they were gazing up like they knew what room we were in. I got up from the bed, and Jimmy moved away from the window, closing the blinds in the process.

I looked over long enough to see everyone's heads craned back, though.

They definitely knew what room we were in.

"It's someone from downstairs," I said.

"What?" Jimmy asked.

"They're all looking up at our balcony. Someone from the front desk gave out our information."

"Then someone from the front desk is about to lose their damn job."

"Jimmy, now isn't the time to react. We need to be proactive. We have to get this situation under control," I said.

Jimmy strode over to me and took me in his arms. His lips crashed to mine, and I could feel his want for me. I gripped his shirt and pulled him into me, savoring his lips against mine.

How I wished we could spend one night together without the worries of the world dancing outside.

"You take the hotel room for the night," he said. "I'll put myself together and leave. Act like I had a meeting or something. I'll make an extra special stop by the front desk to let the manager know I'll be informing the community of their relaxed press policies."

"Jimmy."

"Don't worry. I'll do it with a smile," he said. "In the morning, you can sneak out the back of the hotel, and no one will notice. I'll have my driver waiting back there for you at eight in the morning. Since you're in a fabulous new outfit, you can come to work in that and change. You've got clothes in that rolling wardrobe, right?"

"Yes. And I never thought I would need it, but now I'm glad I have it," I said.

"Don't order from room service. I'll make sure a nice dinner is sent to you tonight along with a bottle of fine wine. I've got chefs around this area I would trust with this kind of thing, but the room service in this hotel I'm not so sure of any longer. Expect dinner around six."

"Will do," I said.

I watched Jimmy get dressed before he kissed me one last time. I wanted him to stay. I wanted him to stay with me, and we could sneak out together. I wanted to tear up this hotel room and use the jacuzzi tub I knew was in the bathroom. I wanted to hold him while we bathed, eat dinner with him, and walk like nothing was going on outside.

Like the world wasn't trying to rip us apart.

Instead, I watched him leave, and it left me wondering if we could really do this. We couldn't even meet at a hotel without being spotted and without the world wondering what debaucheries were taking place. Nowhere was safe and no one was safe, and that meant we weren't safe.

Could I really stay in a relationship with a man if I didn't feel safe?

I sat on the edge of the bed and allowed the tears to come. I didn't try to stop them, and I didn't try to wipe them away. There were moments when things felt perfect, when it felt like the world was finally looking up at us instead of down on us. Then, there were moments like the one I was in when I was sitting in a lonely hotel room shut off from the world with my dress rolled up, hickies on my neck, and an emptiness in the pit of my stomach.

And I was back to wondering if things could really work with us.

Chapter 19

Jimmy

I lay in bed all night wondering what Ashley was doing. Was she using the jacuzzi tub and drinking the wine I sent her? Was she curled up naked in bed and enjoying the plethora of movies on the television for her to watch? Did she enjoy the steak I sent her? What did she think about the crème brûlée?

I hadn't heard from her all last night, so it shouldn't have shocked me when I woke up to an email from her saying she was taking a personal day.

But it hurt.

I felt sick. It seemed like every time I needed her for something, she was taking off, calling in sick when she wasn't sick or taking personal days when I needed her here the most. The investors were floundering and hounding my inbox, and she was needed to keep an eye on balance sheets and transactions that were taking place.

And yet, she was nowhere to be found.

It hurt. And the worst part was, I had no idea why she was avoiding me again or why she wasn't at work when this company was at such a critical point. Yes, I had given her back the laptop so she could remote in, but at this juncture with the company, it was imperative we put up a strong front. Every time she didn't come into work, it made corporate look weak. It stirred up rumors and mutterings between everyone who saw me here but didn't see her. If she wanted the rumors to stop, this wasn't the way to make them stop.

No matter her reason for calling out, I wasn't going to let her slip away this time. I wasn't going to let her back away from me like she had before. We were on good footing, and just because yesterday fell through didn't mean things weren't going to work with us. She was being paranoid. We could make this work. Every company went through rough patches like this, and we needed to find a way to work through the stress.

At least, I kept telling myself that.

"Knock, knock," Trish said.

"What's up?" I asked.

"So, Markus popped back up on the map."

"In China?" I asked.

"Nope. On the other side of Canada. Don't know how he got there, but he's there. He filed for Chapter 11 bankruptcy for his own company."

She tossed the papers onto my desk before she sat down in the chair in front of me.

"So why is he not in handcuffs?" I asked.

"Because he only went in to hand off the paperwork he'd signed. His lawyer is working with him to keep him as off the radar as possible. At least, that's what we assume."

"So, again. Why is he not in handcuffs?"

"Because he only popped up on a camera outside of a store a few minutes after he dropped the signed papers off to his lawyer. He's got a small pad in the scenic area around there that he kept off the books. The house was in the name Lou Roth."

It made me sick to even hear that fucking name.

"The investigators believe he's coming back down to Miami eventually to wipe the rest of his businesses clean and take off. To declare bankruptcy in the US installment of his company, he has to be in the US, specifically, in the state where his headquarters operates."

"So he's coming back," I said.

"That's what the investigators think. But it doesn't look good. He can file from any place in Florida so long as he files in Florida. If he succeeds, he can dissolve, take off to a place with no extradition, and that's that."

I nodded my head as I chewed on the inside of my lip.

"The good news is you shouldn't have to worry about anything being funneled from your company from this point on. Him being forced to liquidate like this means he knows he's been caught."

"That also means we won't see a penny of it back," I said.

"Not necessarily. The assets seized and already frozen by the government will eventually be dispersed. In percentages, of course. It won't cover all he stole, but you'll still see some of that money back."

"Is that all?" I asked.

"That's it," she said.

"Then I have somewhere I need to be. Thank you for stopping by."

I didn't care any longer. I mean, I cared about my company and what was happening, but if Markus was on the run, there was nothing else I could do. Ross was working on getting the FBI the concise, concrete proof they needed while Ashley was running around fuck-knew-where. I had a relationship that meant more to me than life itself that was falling apart, and my time was needed elsewhere.

Everything I could do to help my company was being taken care of.

I ushered Trish out of my office before I locked it behind me. I escorted her down to the parking garage, and we parted ways with a handshake. I got into my car and fought the paparazzi outside to get onto the main road, and then I got lost on some back roads trying to get to Ashley's apartment.

It took me almost an hour to find it, but no one was on my tail because of it.

I parked in the back and made my way in quietly. I took the stairs instead of the elevator all the way up to the fourteenth floor. I hoped she was there. I hoped she was simply taking time to herself. I hoped there wasn't some grand emergency with Cass or her mother or another facet of her life that was being dropped on her shoulders.

I wasn't sure if she would be able to handle anything else.

I knocked on the door and heard shuffling behind it. I heard the little pitter-patter of puppy feet before the doorknob turned. The door cracked open and Ashley was standing there, her eyes scanning me frightfully.

"It's only me," I said. "I wanted to come check on you."

"I took a personal day, not a sick day," she asked.

"I know. I still wanted to make sure you were okay and that you got out of the hotel all right."

"Yep. I'm good," she said.

"May I come in?"

She was hesitant, but she opened the door and let me in. She had the blinds drawn on her apartment, and the porch door was locked. Her favorite part of this entire fucking place and she couldn't even enjoy it.

It made my gut spark with anger.

"I'm worried about you," I said.

"Nothing to worry about. Just needed a personal day."

"We need you at the company. For a strong front," I said.

"Then you should have told me the personal day couldn't be granted."

"I was concerned something might've happened at the hotel or you were holed up in here because of the paparazzi."

"I would've told you that if I was," she said.

"I had another meeting with my lawyer this morning."

"How did it go?"

I watched her cross the room and lean against her kitchen table like she was trying to put distance between us. She pulled a cardigan tightly around her, and I stuffed my hands into my pockets. I wanted to come off as calm as I could, though I knew something was wrong.

Something was bothering her about us.

"If I tell you, will you tell me what's wrong?" I asked.

"Sure," she said with a shrug.

"Markus was spotted on the other side of Canada. He had a private place on the other coastline under the name Lou Roth."

"Fucking asshat," Ashley said.

"Yeah. He filed for bankruptcy and dissolved everything. The investigators think he's headed to Florida to do the same thing here."

"Then he'll take off, and we'll never see him again."

"Essentially."

"What did your lawyer say to do about it?"

"Nothing. It was merely an update. Ross is getting the numbers together and formalizing all the proof in case we can get him into court, but it's not as clear-cut as I thought it might be."

"Never is," she said.

"My lawyer says we shouldn't have anything else to worry about."

"I'm not so sure about that."

"With Markus, I meant."

Her eyes connected with mine as her head slowly nodded.

"Talk to me," I said. "Communicate with me."

"I had to sneak out of the back of a hotel this morning to cover your ass," Ashley said.

I knew immediately where I had fucked up the moment she said it.

"I'm sorry. I thought with it being such a nice room, you might've enjoyed—"

"Exactly. You assumed something. Instead of talking with me about how I would feel about something like that, you told me that was what was happening."

"In my defense, though I'm sure it'll anger you, you did ask me last night what I wanted to do about it. It was the first thing that popped into my mind, so I rolled with it."

"You're right. It does make me angry. It shouldn't be an issue that you're constantly falling apart at the seams, and I'm angry about it. I can't be everyone's totem pole to lean on. This is affecting me too. Have you seen the news?"

"Why does everyone keep asking me that?"

"Because it's important, Jimmy. They're dissecting my life. They're talking about my mother."

"Wait a second. What?" I asked

"Yeah. They're talking about my mother with Alzheimer's like it's morning coffee time with the family. They're saying I'm screwing around with my boss to get my mind off the fact that I won't have a family after she passes. Like my life is for their public consumption, Jimmy!"

"I'm sorry," I said. "Ashley, tell me what I can do."

"I don't know what you can do. I don't know if there's anything we can do. I don't know if this is possible, and I don't know if we could ever be happy, and I don't know if me working for you is smart. I don't know who to trust or who to talk to or where to go when I get to work because I feel like I'm being watched everywhere I go. I don't know how much longer my mother is going to live, and I don't know if I can keep sneaking around with you, and I sure as hell don't know if this will ever settle."

I took a step toward Ashley before she took two steps back.

"I fucked up, and I'm sorry," I said. "I should have had the sense about me to ask you how you felt about that plan, but it wasn't only to save my ass. It was to make sure you were covered too."

"Well, your efforts are fruitless because they're still devouring me on the morning and evening news."

"What can I do?" I asked.

"You can leave," she said.

I felt my stomach drop to my toes as her eyes connected with mine.

"For fuck's sake, Jimmy. I'm not breaking up with you, but if you think I can hold you and my mother up along with trying to keep some shred of secrecy and decency to my life away from the hands of the press, you're sorely mistaken. I know you're hurting right now, but I can't come to you because you're hurting too."

"I can be strong for you, Ashley. I can be strong for us both for a while."

"I don't know if you can," she said breathlessly.

Watching tears crest her eyes without being able to go to her shattered my heart. I felt like I was bleeding nonstop and nothing I did helped with the pain. She sniffled and sat down into a chair, her face falling into her hand.

She looked so tired and worn down. All I wanted to do was try to make it better, but in the process, I was making it worse.

"Please, leave," Ashley said.

"Will I see you tomorrow?" I asked.

"If I don't take another personal day, yes," she said.

"Please come into work. We need you."

"Yeah. It seems everyone does."

I slowly walked toward her door as her head lifted from her hands. Her eyes were tired, and her shoulders were slumped. She looked like she had aged ten years over the course of the past three weeks. My hand fell onto her doorknob, and I moved as slowly as I could. Hoping she could call for me and tell me to come back. Tell me to stay. Tell me to sit with her and hold her while she cried.

But the tears fell down her cheeks as I slipped out the door. Unnoticed and unnecessary.

Chapter 20

Ashley

"You know I love you, right?" Cass asked.

"I love you too," I said.

"So you know what I'm about to say comes from a place of love, right?"

"What is it?" I asked.

"You need to grow the fuck up."

My jaw went slack as my eyes widened.

"What?" I asked flatly.

"You, Ashley Ternbeau, need to grow the fuck up."

"What are you talking about?"

"It's Friday. This is your second personal day since you started questioning things *again* between you and Jimmy."

"So? I'm working from home. I haven't slacked on any of my work."

"You're being a coward."

"I'm being sensible," I said.

"No, you're not. The company you work for is tanking, and they're looking to you for guidance. You and Jimmy and whoever the hell else works on that top floor. But you're sitting here, running from your problems like a teenage girl."

"You're being unreasonable."

"I'm being unreasonable? You agreed to the hotel, Ashley! When he called you up and said 'meet me there,' you fucking dressed yourself to the nines for some slinky little vacation hook-up. And then you got pissed when it didn't happen because people followed you? Do you know how hypocritical and childish that sounds?"

"He wanted me to stay there and sneak out to cover his ass."

"But you were willing to sneak in and hop on his dick?" she asked. "You're as guilty as Jimmy is for all this. What did you think was going to happen when you started doing this with him?"

"I didn't think I would end up on the cover of a tabloid magazine!"

"Oh, really? You didn't know that the man who is always photographed whenever he goes out would be photographed with you whenever you two went out? What, you didn't think the media would like the fact that a tech mogul billionaire was screwing one of his corporate coworkers?"

"No, I didn't think this would happen!"

"Then you're an idiot," she said.

"I think one of the requirements of my job is the strict fact that I'm not an idiot," I said.

"A social idiot. Right now, you're pissed that the rules of social engagement apply to you. You're pissed the media is devouring the fact that you're sleeping with your boss when you curl up in this apartment every night and watch the same bullshit pop culture swill that now has your face plastered all over it."

"You can stop now," I said.

"No, because you're still sitting here. It's time to buck up and face facts. You love him. I know it. You've told me, and I can see it in your eyes whenever you talk about him. He's going through a hard time, just like you are, and you need to be there for him."

"Well, he needs to be there for me too."

"And he was. You told me he came to check up on you, and you threw him out."

"I didn't throw him out. I asked him to leave."

"In your world, that's throwing someone out," she said. "But the point is, he was here. Being strong for you. Asking you what was wrong. You pushed him away when all he wanted to do was help you like you've helped him. You don't get to be angry at him because all of this is your doing."

"Thanks for taking my side."

"This isn't about taking sides, Ash. This is about you being a fucking adult when the man at your side needs you to be," she said. "You need to realize all of this before you lose him for good."

"I don't know what to do, Cass."

"Well, the answer isn't going to come to you when you're cooped up in your apartment. You need to lean on one another instead of running away from each other. From him. Tell him how you feel."

"Why should I be the one to make that first move?"

"Because it's the twenty-first century, and men are allowed to have feelings, which means women are allowed to take the first step. Right now, the ball's in your fucking court because he came to see you and you asked him to leave. It's not his move to make anymore. It's yours. He already made his move, and you wanted to be alone instead."

I clenched my jaw as I stared at the curtain-covered sliding glass door.

"It's written all over your face, Ashley. Even when you're angry with him, you're passionately angry. You don't just love him. You're in love with him, and sometimes it isn't on the man's shoulders to make the first move. Sometimes, it's simply in the woman's court. That's not a bad thing, but it is a thing. So you need to stop making excuses and start conducting yourself like an adult before you lose him. Even men like him know when they've had enough and know when they're not wanted."

"I wanted some time to wrap my head around things."

"News flash. Adults don't always get that," Cass said.

And I knew she was right.

I stood up and hugged my friend before I went to get dressed for work. I wasn't going to be in until after lunch, but it didn't matter. If people weren't staring at me because I was late, they would be staring at me because I was fucking Jimmy. I drove myself to work and ignored the looks of people as I walked through the hallways.

I needed to talk with Jimmy, even if it looked bad that I was in his office.

I went straight for his office, but I saw it was dark. I knocked on his door anyway, hoping he was simply resting his eyes. I could feel everyone's eyes on me as I clutched my coffee, my hand lightly knocking against the door.

"He hasn't shown up yet."

I turned my eyes to see Ross as his voice hit my ears.

"Is everything okay?" I asked.

"Yep. Just taking a day out of the office."

"Do you know when he'll be back?"

"Did he know when you were going to be back?" he asked.

I furrowed my brow as Ross nodded his head.

"My office?" he asked.

"Sure," I said. "No problem."

I walked behind Ross and shut the door behind us. He dropped the folder in his hands and leaned against his desk. I felt my stomach clenching with nervousness as the look in his eye grew stern.

Had something happened while I was gone?

"Jimmy isn't here because he's working. He's out there, trying to talk with our investors and fix things."

"Is there anything I can do?" I asked. "If he's with the investors, I should be there, right?"

"It's not a monetary meeting, so no," he said. "But there is something I want to say to you."

"Okay. Shoot."

"If you couldn't handle the heat, you shouldn't have come back."

I felt my stomach drop to the floor as I swallowed hard.

"Jimmy's here every day, despite the media and despite the hounding and despite everything falling apart. He's here because he knows how important appearances are in a corporate atmosphere. He's here trying to fix your reputation and his reputation and the company's reputation. Meanwhile, you're at home, remoting in to do the bare minimum required of you in the hopes you can skirt by in the shadows."

I had no idea what to say to defend myself.

"Ashley, you're a smart woman. Better with numbers than anyone I've ever come across. But your job is more than that. Working for corporate is more than that. It's about strength and determination, gritting your teeth and smiling, even when the wolves are drooling in your face. No one's going to tell you when you have to come in or when you have to leave, not because you can come and go as you please, but because we're all adults. We know what's expected of us in a work atmosphere."

I blinked my tears away and cleared my throat.

"I was the one who put you up for this promotion, and I was the one that supported Jimmy's relationship with you when he came clean to me about it. But now that the two of you are in the crosshairs of the media, you're leaving him to deal with a mess the two of you should be dealing with together."

"I didn't look at it that way," I said.

"I know you didn't. Otherwise, you'd be at work instead of wherever the hell you've been."

"I'm sorry, Ross."

"Don't apologize to me. I'm not the one in love with you."

"What?" I asked.

"Jimmy cares about you. A lot. And he's willing to go to hell and back to fix what's going on, with his company and with your reputation. No matter what it does to his. But all I see is another woman not willing to put up the fight he's putting up, and I'm concerned."

"It's not like that."

"Then prove it to me. Don't just say it. Get out there and show me. Show him. Show all of us. All these rumors around the office? They aren't about you two sneaking around together."

"They're not?" I asked.

"No. They're about how you aren't good enough for him. How he deserves better. How you're a rebound from Nina and nothing else. And I've been trying to interject and squash them as I can, but I want you to know those rumors aren't on unstable ground. Your actions are proving them right."

I bit down on the inside of my cheek as my jaw began to quiver.

"In a corporate world, appearances are everything, especially during scandals like the one Markus brought down on our heads. But in the world Jimmy lives in, personal conviction is everything. You say you care about him, but your actions say otherwise."

"Is that all?" I asked.

"If you can't handle this, then that's fine. Most people can't handle working in a corporate atmosphere. But what you need to do if you can't handle it is wait for the dust to settle and then step down quietly."

"I tried that, you know," I said. "I sent him an email saying I quit, but he didn't process the paperwork with HR. That was his choice."

"But when he offered you this position, you came back. You stepped back into this office and back into this role. Own up to the choices you made and stop trying to make it seem like someone else made them for you."

"You have no idea what my life is like outside of these walls, Ross. The shit I deal with and the pressure I'm under."

"We all have lives outside of these walls. That doesn't mean you get to slack behind these walls," he said.

I tried to keep from crying, but a tear streaked my cheek anyway.

"You're a wonderful woman, Ashley, an intelligent woman. Stop being so scared."

I closed my eyes and turned my back on him as I opened his office door.

I stormed down the hallway, rushing by the receptionist's desk. I slammed into my office and locked the door behind me. I tossed my coffee into the trash can and tossed my shit into the corner. Then, I flopped down into my leather seat and put my head on my desk.

I was going to have a good cry. I was going to sob as loud as I needed to. I was going to let the tears pour, and then I was going to splash some water in my face.

Then, I was going to pull up my pants and keep going. Then, I was going to do exactly what was asked of me. Because as much as I hated to admit to any of it, they were right.

Chapter 21

Jimmy

I was sitting on the porch of my beach house overlooking the ocean. The silence was comforting, and the alone time was necessary. I left my phone and my laptop behind, erasing the world in Miami as I stared out into the horizon.

I couldn't remember the last time silence had been so welcomed.

I needed some time to get away from everything and think. I had so many people chirping constantly in my ear, and it was drowning out my own thoughts and emotions. I was trying to keep all these damn balls in the air, and they kept crashing down as soon as I got a good rhythm going. The sound of the ocean ebbing against the shoreline soothed me, and my mind fell blank as I leaned into my chair.

I'd had a long talk with my lawyer before I left. Trish thought we were in a good place with the investigation. The prosecuting attorney was tacking onto the charges already filed, which was something we could do since Markus wasn't in custody yet. There was a warrant out for his arrest for the other charges, and he was now officially on the FBI's watch list and Do Not Fly list. She felt we were in a good place to catch him and nail him to the wall, and that gave me some sort of peace.

Then, there was Ashley.

I didn't know what the hell I was going to do with that woman. She drove me nuts, but she provided me with the greatest relief I'd ever felt in my life. When I was with her, nothing else mattered. When I was gazing into her eyes, nothing else existed. My heart fluttered in my chest whenever I heard her voice, and my body caved to her every time her lips connected with mine.

I loved her. I was in love with Ashley Ternbeau.

I had to figure out a way to fix our image in the media, but I wanted to be authentic about it. I didn't want to force something that wasn't there. Presenting a united front was a must, but we couldn't do that if she wasn't coming to work.

I couldn't blame her. She was thrust into a social situation she didn't understand. It took me years to navigate the social world of the business industry. It took me years to cultivate the image I had and to manipulate the mainstream media to suit the tone of my company. Ashley didn't understand any of that. She was a numbers woman. No one would expect her to understand.

I pictured Ashley in my mind, and it drew a smile across my cheeks. My stomach clenched with happiness and butterflies were flapping in my chest. I'd never felt this strongly about a woman before. I'd never wanted to fight so badly for a woman before. At any other point in my life, once the media caught wind of a relationship, I would've dropped her. I would've broken up with her so I didn't have to deal with the bullshit that came with the cameras and the rumors and the following us around to catch us kissing shit the paparazzi did.

But with Ashley, it was worth it. With Ashley, I kind of wanted it.

I wanted the world to know she was mine and she was at my side. I wanted them to see her the way I did. For her beauty and her intelligence and her strength. She had so much sitting on her shoulders, and people were asking her for more than she knew how to give. But instead of letting me help her, she was pushing me away, and it hurt.

I opened my eyes and drew in the salty air. The sun was hanging high in the sky, and I allowed myself to bask in it. Ashley would've loved coming out here with me again, but it was tainted for her. I had to fix things with us and with the press before I could offer to bring her back.

I knew her well enough to know she'd look over her shoulder if I didn't.

I closed my eyes again and saw Ashley again. Only this time, she was in a white dress, strapless and clinging to her body as the satin fabric fell to the floor. She had something covering her face and I looked down, seeing the decadent tuxedo I had on.

I felt my heart clench at the sight of her.

Those pouty red lips and the bouquet of flowers in her hands. The heels she walked gracefully in and how her hips swayed against the fabric of her dress. Ross was standing at my side, and Cass was in front of me, and Ashley was slowly coming down an aisle.

I could hardly breathe, she was so beautiful.

I ripped my eyes open and almost fell back in my chair. What the hell had I just seen? I looked down at my left hand, and for a split second, I could see a ring there. The outline of a wedding ring Ashley was sliding onto my finger.

I ran down the stairs and got into my car. I rode into a small town that sat right outside of Miami. I came across a quaint little jewelry store, and I pulled into the parking lot.

A peace unlike none other fell over my body.

I'd never felt this way before. I'd never considered marrying any woman, but seeing Ashley in that dress and looking at that ring for a split second on my finger settled something inside of me, tugged at a part of me I didn't think existed. I got out of the car and went into the jewelry shop, intent on simply looking.

But the longer I looked, the more drawn I was to one specific ring.

It had Ashley written all over it. The band was small, and the diamond was of a very clear quality. It was cut into the shape of a heart and had two aquamarine stones sitting off to the side. It came with a matching wedding band, whose stones alternated between the clear, shimmering diamond and the glittering aquamarine stone, like the color of the ocean reflected in her emerald eyes. I couldn't take my eyes off it. It was like it was made for her.

"Looking at rings?"

I clenched my jaw as her voice wafted over my ears. Was the universe hell-bent on making my life a living nightmare? I tried to ignore her, and I kept looking at rings, walking around the store and trying to get away from her.

But Nina was fucking following me like always.

"For what it's worth, I'm sorry Jimmy."

My movements ceased, but I refused to look up at her. To give her the time of day. To give her the energy of my focusing on her.

She didn't deserve any of it, but I did deserve her apology.

"I'm sorry for all of the issues I caused and the hurt I brought into your life."

I continued to bite my tongue, but I could tell she wasn't finished.

"I'm seeing a therapist," Nina said. "You know, working out my issues and all. I've got a long way to go, but he thinks I should have a fresh start somewhere. That I'm ready for it."

My eyes were scanning the jewelry mindlessly, but I wasn't paying attention to any of it.

"California's a lot like here, but you know, with none of the people I've hurt. I'm moving out there in a couple of months. My therapist wants to have a few more sessions before I leave."

I continued moving along, my eyes resting on some pointless watches and some gaudy necklaces.

"I hope the two of you have a good life together, Jimmy."

And honestly? I did too.

Nina sighed and turned away from me before she walked to the other end of the jewelry store. I went back over to the rings, my eyes falling to the one that reminded me of Ashley. I looked up into a mirror and saw Nina at the door, her eyes connecting with mine through the reflection. The two of us stood there for a moment with nothing but commemorative silence passing between us.

Then she pushed through the front door and left.

I was glad she was leaving. She wouldn't be around any longer for any of us to run into. We wouldn't have to put up with her bullshit or see her out at dinner or run into her randomly in town. I felt a massive weight being lifted from my shoulders as my hand rested on top of the glass.

"Can I help you with anything, sir?"

"Yes," I said. "I would like this aquamarine wedding band set, please."

"Ah, that's a good one. It's been here a while. I'm surprised no one's picked it up until now," he said.

"Because it was waiting for me," I said plainly. "Could you box them up separately? And put the engagement ring in a black velvet box."

"I can do that, sir. Is there anything else you want?" he asked.

"Nope," I said. "Just put it on my card."

"Right away, sir. And congratulations," he said.

I nodded my head as he walked away, watching as he wrapped everything up. He swiped my card and handed me a receipt, but I bunched it up and threw it away. I didn't care to know how much it cost, and if Ashley said no, it would still be hers to keep. That ring was made for her. Meant for her and only her. She could pawn it for money if she didn't want it, but it wasn't coming back here.

Not when it reflected the beauty of her face every time I looked at it.

Chapter 22

Ashley

I was sitting at my desk when a familiar pair of footsteps started falling on the carpet. Everyone fell quiet out in the hallway as Jimmy walked up to his office. I looked up and saw him, with his confident form and his stoic face, unlocking his office with a big coffee in his hand. He was in an all-black suit, from his tie to his socks. He hair was swooped back, and he seemed a little more rested. It made me smile as I watched him walk into his office.

Then, the phone on my desk rang.

"Ashley Ternbeau."

"Come into my office, please," Jimmy said.

He hung up the phone, and I looked up into the hallway. People were staring at me, and that was when I saw his office door hanging wide open. Everyone had probably heard what he had said to me, and they were all waiting to see what I would do.

But I couldn't let them control my actions any longer. What was done was done, and if Jimmy needed to see me, then he would see me.

I smoothed my hands over my pencil skirt and started out of my office. I walked into his, and when he looked up at me, he gestured for me to close the door. I furrowed my brow as I turned around, watching people gape as I closed them off from the view.

Then, the hustling and bustling began again.

"First off, I owe you an apology," Jimmy said.

"For what?" I asked.

"For not speaking with you over the weekend."

"You have a life. That's nothing to apologize for," I said.

"You're a part of that life personally. I should have called you and told you where I was, and for not communicating with you after demanding you do it with me, I'm sorry. It made me a hypocrite."

"I haven't been the best partner either, as Cass and Ross have brought to my attention. So I think an apology from me is in order as well."

"I'm also apologizing on behalf of Ross. What he said to you was unprofessional, at best. He was speaking to you as my friend in a professional atmosphere, and I'm not happy with him about it."

"But it didn't make what he said any less true. Cass gave me a bit of the same lecture before I came to work. I can only figure you're as fed up with my antics as they are," I said.

"I could never be fed up with you, Ashley. Frustrated, sure. Worried, yes. But fed up? Never."

I looked up into his eyes as he relaxed against his desk. He crossed his ankles and was fiddling with something in his pocket. My eyes dropped to the movement, and it stopped immediately. I furrowed my brow in confusion.

"Is something wrong?" I asked.

"I went back to the beach house this weekend to get away for a bit," Jimmy said. "I needed some time to clear my head and think things through."

"I know how that feels."

"I know you do. This scenario you've been thrust into isn't fair. You aren't a press woman. You're a numbers woman. And no one can expect you to know how to navigate something like this so quickly into your corporate career."

"Doesn't excuse that me working from home was basically running from the problem instead of facing it head-on."

"I care about you, Ashley. A lot."

"I care about you, too, Jimmy."

"I don't think you understand how much, though," he said.

His eyes fell to his lap as I took a step toward him.

"What's on your mind?" I asked. "I get the feeling you didn't call me in here to talk about something professional."

"I've been thinking a lot about how to handle the press and about how to get our images back on track without having to lie to them any longer."

"Or at least make it seem like we aren't trying to sneak around," I said. "Because I think they know by now we were lying."

"I lied."

"We lied," I said. "Jimmy, Ross was right about one thing. I've been leaving you to do this on your own, and that's not right. We got into this situation together, so we should be navigating it together. Instead, I've been curled up in my apartment so afraid someone will corner me on the street or find me in another parking garage that I didn't stop to consider that I was leaving you alone to deal with this."

"I get it. Ashley, I understand. I was there once too. Navigating the media and using them to benefit my company and my image is something I do well now because I used to not do it well. I had time to learn. Years, in fact. You've had weeks, and even that time frame is generous."

"So, you're not mad at me?" I asked.

"No, Ashley. I'm not mad at you. In fact ..."

I watched his arm move from his pocket as he clenched something in his fist. Before I could see what it was, a rapid knock came at his door.

"I'm really sorry, Miss Ternbeau, but I have a call for you."

I furrowed my brow as Jimmy jammed his fist back into his pocket. I opened the door, and the receptionist was standing there with her corded telephone stretched all the way across the hallway. My heart was slamming in my chest, but I didn't know why. I looked back at Jimmy and saw him shaking his head, like he was upset at something.

What in the world did Jimmy have in his hand?

"Who is it?" I asked.

"The nursing home. The lady on the line says it's urgent," the receptionist said.

I ripped the phone from her hand and held it up to my ear.

"Hello? Who is this?" I asked.

"Ashley. Thank heavens. You need to get down to the nursing home."

"Why? What's wrong?" I asked.

"Your mother's come down with pneumonia, and with her Alzheimer's worsening, her body isn't handling it well."

"What do you mean? How long has she been sick?" I asked.

I looked over at Jimmy, and he pushed himself off his desk.

"It happened late last night. Came down with a fever, and we gave her some Tylenol to combat it. She kept coughing through the night, so one of the nurses ordered some late-night tests. Fluid is still gathering, and her immune system is too compromised with her Alzheimer's to keep up. Please, Ashley. You need to get down here."

I thrust the phone into the receptionist's chest and ran to my office. I gathered my things as my hands began to tremble. Tears rose quickly to my eyes and rushed down my cheeks, and as soon as I whipped up, I felt a pair of hands on my shoulders.

Jimmy turned me around to look up at him, and the waterworks unleashed.

"I've already called my driver. He'll meet you downstairs. Go, Ashley. My driver will take you anywhere you need to go."

I threw my arms around him and kissed his cheek repeatedly. I didn't care who saw or who snapped pictures to sell to some bullshit magazine. I kissed him all over his cheeks before capturing his lips, and he wrapped his arms around me. I hoped he felt it. I hoped the love and appreciation I had for him bled from my skin and soaked into his. I pulled away from him and ran down the hallway, yelling for someone to hold the elevator door.

I shuffled on my feet all the way down to the parking garage.

Jimmy's driver was there with an open door. I leaped into the car, and when he got to the driver's seat, he squealed tires trying to get out of the parking garage. The paparazzi were thicker than ever, and we almost hit a couple of people, trying to get out to the road.

Served them fucking right if they got hit.

My hands were shaking as I pulled out my phone. I texted Cass what was going on and told her to be on standby. I didn't know what was happening, but I knew I would need her.

Something told me in my gut that I would need her.

The car pulled into the nursing home, and I slammed out of it. I ran in my heels through the front doors, and a nurse caught me by the arm. She took my hand, and we raced down the opposite direction, away from my mother's room and into the medical attachment the nursing home had right there on the grounds.

The moment I ran into my mother's room, my back hit the wall.

My mother was withered away to almost nothing, even though I'd seen her only a week ago. Her mouth was hanging open, and she was coughing, struggling to take even shallow breaths. She was gurgling like she was underwater as my eyes scanned the monitors.

Her fever was one hundred and four and still climbing.

"Can't you give her something for it?" I asked.

"We already have. We can't give her body any more. Her liver will crash otherwise," the nurse said.

I watched my mother struggle to turn her head.

"Who are you?" she asked.

I whimpered as I walked toward her, pulling up a chair so I could sit down.

"Oh, Mom," I said.

"Mom? I'm not your mother," she said.

I took her hand anyway.

She didn't fight me. At least, she was too weak to fight. Usually, she did. If she didn't remember who I was, she fought any touch I wanted to give her, but she was immobile in her bed as her eyes stared up at the ceiling. Still, her fever ticked higher.

I brought my mother's hand to my lips, and the beeping of her heart monitor went up. I felt my mother's hand shaking, and I settled it back onto the bed. I leaned over and pressed a wet kiss to my mother's cheek, and I heard her heart rate skyrocket.

"Come on. We need you out of the room," the nurse said.

"She's my mother. I'm not going anywhere," I said.

I tried to shrug the nurse off, but she had a strong grip on my arm.

"She doesn't recognize you, and the stress on her heart is too much," the nurse said.

"I'm her damn daughter!" I said.

My mother's heart rate was off-the-charts as doctors flooded the room. I watched them stabilize her as the nurse rubbed my back. Tears poured down my cheeks as my entire body shook.

My mother was dying, and she had no idea who I was.

I watched the doctor's give her something in her IV before they left the room. Her eyes fluttered closed, and her vitals steadied out. Her fever was still growing, but they had ice packs all around her body, trying to get her to cool down without pumping her body full of medication any longer.

She had probably built up a tolerance to them over the years.

"How long?" I asked.

"Honestly?" the nurse asked.

"Yep."

"I'll be shocked if she makes it through the night."

I leaned my forehead against the glass as my mother slipped off to sleep. My heart shattered into a million pieces. The last of my family was about to slip away from me. Then, I would be an orphan. No more Thanksgiving dinners and no more Christmas presents to bring her. No more laughter when she was lucid and no one to travel down memory lane with.

My mother was dying, and I would be all alone.

"Could I go in? Now that she's asleep?" I asked.

The nurse looked hesitant, and I drew in a deep breath.

"I'll be quiet, I promise."

"Then, go ahead, sweetheart. Take your time," she said.

I opened the door and slipped in silently. I pulled up the chair again and took my mother's hand in mine. I brought it to my lips and kissed it repeatedly, memorizing how it felt. I interlocked our hands together, feeling the way our fingers mimicked one another's. I reached up and wiped some hair from her face, memorizing how it felt underneath my skin.

So many small things I wouldn't get to feel again.

What was I going to do without her?

I thought about all the things she'd never see. The grandchildren she would never have and the wedding she would never witness. She wouldn't be there for the birth of my children or any of their birthdays. She wouldn't be able to run around in the yard with them or take pictures on their first birthday. She wouldn't be there to give my fiancé the rundown on what she would do to him if he hurt me.

She wouldn't even be there to ogle over the ring he would get for me.

Silent tears poured down my face as I rested my head against the mattress. One last nap with my mother. That was all I had. I closed my eyes and allowed myself to drift off, and so many memories came to mind. The first time I could remember hugging my mother. The first time I could remember her kissing me. The first time she ever told me she was proud of me and the way she rejoiced with me when I was accepted into college.

I saw all of them flashing behind my eyes as I slept.

I groaned and shifted as my eyes fluttered open. The sun had set outside, and the faint beeping of the machines brought me back to life.

My mother's heart rate was steadily dropping, and her fever was still raging at one hundred and five degrees.

She was dying, and I wasn't sure I was strong enough to be around for it.

I stood up on shaky legs and bent over to kiss her lips. I nuzzled our noses together, taking in the feel of her one last time. I released her hand and brought it up to her cheek, cupping it before I ran my fingers through her hair.

"I love you so much, Mom. I swear, I'll never forget you. Not for a second."

I picked up my things and left the room as the machines began to drone behind me. I refused to turn my head around. I refused to remember my mother like that, hooked up to tubes and lying lifeless on a hospital bed in a nursing home.

I refused to debase her legacy with that mental image.

Nurses and doctors were running past me as I walked up the hallway. I held my head high as tears streamed down my neck. I turned and walked out the front doors and continued walking into the street, not really going anywhere except for forward.

A car pulled up behind me, and a pair of strong hands settled on my shoulders, turning me around as the darkness of Jimmy's car called to me. I was led by a pair of warm hands as I got into the car, and as I looked up, I was met with a familiar pair of eyes.

"Oh, Ashley," Cass said. "Come here."

I felt someone slide in beside me as the car pulled off. I wrapped my arms around my best friend as she knelt between my legs. She rocked me side to side as I sobbed in her hair, crying for my mother and yet somehow relieved she was no longer confined to the hell she was living in.

The car pulled away from the nursing home and out onto the main road, and I felt that same strong hand fall to my back. I turned my head to see who was next to me.

And I found the eyes of the man I loved staring down at me.

"Back to your place?" Jimmy asked. Then, he nodded at his driver as his hand found mine, our fingers linking together in strength.

Replacing the feel of my mother's.

Chapter 23

Jimmy

I knew the moment Ashley left work in tears that something was very wrong with her mother. She slammed her way through everyone and was yelling at someone to hold the elevator. I looked at my receptionist, and she had tears in her eyes, tears of sorrow for something she couldn't even understand. I could feel the entire mood on our level change in that moment, and everyone turned their eyes toward me to see what I would do next.

I went back to my office and closed my door.

I sent my driver a text message, telling him to come get me once he dropped Ashley off. Then I set to work trying to track down a way to contact Cassidy. I only knew her first name, but I figured she would be easy to track down anyway. I called in a favor to the private investigator we were using and told him I would owe him a favor if he did something for me.

And twenty minutes later, I had Cassidy's phone number.

"Whoever the hell this is, I can't—"

"It's Jimmy Sheldon," I said.

"What?" she asked. "Who?"

"Jimmy Sheldon. The man attempting to date your best friend."

"Attempt is actually a good word for it," she said. "I still can't talk to you. I have to get to—"

"I know something isn't right with Ashley's mother, and I know it's not good."

"Are you going to let me get a word in edgewise?" she asked.

"No, but I know she's going to want you next to her. I'm packing up my things and headed down to meet my driver in the garage. Can we come pick you up?"

"Where are we going, Mr. FancyPants?"

"To wherever Ashley is. She's going to want her best friend once she's done," I said.

I gathered up my things and placed them into my briefcase as Cassidy fell silent.

"I'm in front of Ashley's apartment."

"I'll be there in fifteen to get you," I said.

I hung up the phone and told my receptionist to cancel my day. She tried to fight me, but I walked around the corner before I could hear it. Ross stuck his head out of the office to question me, but I held up my hand to silence him.

I still wasn't happy with him, and I wasn't in the mood to have a conversation.

I took the elevator down to the garage and met my driver there. He whisked me through the growing crowd of people in front of my office and took me straight to Ashley's apartment. I opened the door for a young woman standing on the sidewalk in front of OceanHomes, and as soon as she slid in, I knew I had the right girl.

"Nice to finally meet the mystery man. Though I have to say, I have a lot to say to you."

"I'm sure you do. I haven't been in good form lately," I said.

"Then at least you recognize it. But I'll say this: Ashley isn't innocent in all this either. She tends to create these storms then act like she didn't tornado all over her life."

"I'm familiar with the type," I said.

"Ashley's a good girl."

"She's a good woman."

"And I think her mom is dying."

I whipped my head around to face her friend as Cass heaved a heavy sigh.

"It's been coming for a while, but Ashley was frantic in her text messages. The words were misspelled and sent at rapid-fire pacing. She said I needed to be at her apartment because she would need me no matter how this ended."

"Shit," I said.

"So, I'll keep the best friend rant to this one phrase: Ashley cares for you. A lot. She deserves better than the way you've been treating her. She's strong, but she's not immovable. Take care of her, and she'll take care of you. But rarely does she take the first step, though it's not for lack of trying to get her to."

"She's stubborn, and I love it."

Cass whipped her eyes up to me as a grin crossed my face.

The two of us rode to the nursing home and sat out there for hours. The sun was starting to set before we saw Ashley emerge from the doors. She was in a trance, and tears were flowing down her cheeks. My heart fell to my toes as I got out of the car. She wasn't looking where she was going, simply walking until something stopped her from doing so.

I stood in front of her, but she looked right through me, so I used my hands to guide her into the car.

The ride back to her apartment was solemn, at best. I didn't care about the media or the investigation or if anyone saw us. By the look on Ashley's face, she had just lost her mother. With the way she was gripping Cassidy and the way she was gripping my hand, she had lost the one thing that kept her rooted to the floor. I sat there, tall and strong, as she volleyed between hugging her best friend and leaning against me.

I wanted to take the pain away from her, shoulder it as my own burden so she could keep on smiling that beautiful smile that always lit up a room.

The driver pulled us up to the curb of her apartment, and I helped her out. I picked her up into my arms and told my driver I'd catch a cab home. I watched him drive off as Cassidy stood at my side, Ashley's arms wrapped around my neck.

"Let's get you upstairs," I said.

She cried into my neck the entire way up, all the way down the hallway, and all the way into her apartment. I sat down on her couch with her in my lap, and her friend brought her some water to drink. She couldn't even take a sip without choking on it.

"Take it slowly," Cassidy said. "Drink it slow."

"I can't believe she's—"

"Ssshh." I said as I stroked her hair. "Take your time."

"What am I supposed to do?" Ashley asked.

"Take it one millisecond at a time," Cassidy said. "I'll be here every step of the way."

"We both will," I said.

"How did you?"

Ashley sighed as her forehead fell against my chest.

"I'll always be here when you need me the most," I said. "No matter what."

"My mom's dead," Ashley said breathlessly.

I wrapped her up in my arms as Cassidy sat beside us. Ashley was crying so hard, she was heaving into my chest. Her fists were holding my clothes so tightly, she was popping buttons off my shirt, ripping through the fabric with her nails as she clung to me.

"I've got you," I said with a whisper. "I've got you, Ashley."

I'd wanted to propose to Ashley that morning. I'd planned to get down on one knee and tell her how much I loved her, show her how much she meant to me, but I couldn't do it now with something like this looming over our heads. The only thing she would think was that her mother wasn't there to witness something like that, and it would taint the moment.

No. Ashley needed to process and heal before I could propose.

I rocked Ashley on the couch as Cassidy ordered us some Chinese takeout. I tried to get her to let me pay for it, but she was as stubborn as Ashley was. Even more so, if that was possible. Ashley sighed into my chest before she lifted her head to look up at me, and the pain in her eyes broke my heart.

"I don't know how or what you did, but thank you," she said.

"No thanks needed, Ashley. I—"

My phone rang before I had a chance to tell her. I groaned as she shifted off my lap, and I dug my phone out of my pocket. It was Ross. Of course, it was Ross. I had taken a personal fucking day, and he was calling me like it was nothing. I muted the call and turned my attention back to Ashley, but he promptly called back.

"Who is it?" Ashley asked.

"No one important," I said.

"So it's Ross."

"Possibly."

"Take it, Jimmy. It could be serious."

"What could be more serious than the woman I love losing her mother?"

I watched Ashley's face contort as Cassidy gasped in the corner. I clenched my jaw and pulled my ringing phone back out of my pocket. My eyes locked with Ashley's as the stunned expression on her face grew, but I could tell by Ross's voice that he was frantic.

"What is it?" I asked.

"The media. It's out of control. You have to do something, Jimmy."

"What do you expect me to do?" I asked.

"You need to get over here and hold a press conference. One of our secretaries tried to leave, and they fucking blew out one of her tires, stranded her in the middle of that wild pack. I had to send the entire security team out there just to get her out of her damn car."

"Call the police. I'm on my way," I said.

"What's going on?" Ashley asked.

"I'm so sorry," I said. "The press outside of the building is getting worse, and one of our secretaries was almost attacked."

"What?" Cassidy asked.

"You have to go," Ashley said.

"I'm not leaving you."

"Get out of here, and go deal with this," she said. "I get it."

"I want to be here with you. For you," I said.

"And you were. You were there, somehow, when I stumbled out of the nursing home in a daze. You kept me from walking straight into the woods and falling off a cliff or something, Jimmy. Go. But call me when it's done. Let me know you're okay."

I wrapped Ashley in my arms and pulled her in for a kiss. I hoped she felt it. The love I bled through my skin for her. I wiped at her tears and kissed her sniffling nose, and then I set my sights on the next task.

I had to set up a press conference and deal with the bullshit.

I texted Ross and told him to set it up. I caught a cab and told them to drop me within a block from my company. I didn't want anyone else getting hurt or having their property damaged because of all this. I could hear police sirens and see their lights blaring as the cab dropped me off. Then I started the short walk up to the podium that was being set up for me.

The media saw me and came running. My security team sprinted up next to me and surrounded me with protection. Cameras were flashing, and people were sticking microphones in my face. The police were hauling people off in police cars left and right.

Good. I wanted them to know I meant business.

I stood by and waited for the podium to be set up. Then, I took my place on the stage. People fell silent, and police were still cuffing individuals. I held my hand up to silence both the cameras and the few questions still flying at me.

"First of all, I want to address the status of my secretary. She's shaken up, but she hasn't been harmed. Thanks to your antics, however, I will be finding out who caused the damage to her vehicle and your company will be supplying her with another one. As well as being slapped with multiple harassment lawsuits."

Murmurs ricocheted through the crowd as I cleared my throat.

"Second of all, the picture circulating of Miss Ternbeau and me is, in fact, real."

That really kicked up the crowd and cameras began flashing again.

"I lied in my prior address to the media to protect her from the hounds I know you all to be. I was dealing with an internal fraud issue, which is being resolved as we speak by the FBI. I didn't want her reputation devoured in the press, but it seems all of you are hell-bent on destroying that young woman's life. So I will come clean."

I drew in a deep breath and hoped Ashley didn't hate me for this later.

"Ashley and I are in love. Deeply in love. She lights up my world in ways you cannot imagine, and she brings an intelligence and a grace to my corporation it has never seen before. Miss Ternbeau, the one you guys have called—what was it?—a 'slut who sucked her way to the top?' She was the one who pointed out the fraud to me in the first place. She was the one who not only put the clues together but found out who was committing the fraud. That intelligent mind of hers saved not only my companies but many more companies who I assume will come forward eventually to talk about this dishonorable man who will never see the light of day again because of the hurt he has caused and the money he has stolen."

The media fell silent, and I saw their microphones waver.

"The investigation is being handled properly and with a quiet demeanor. It has affected many local companies I know all of you have come to love. The business industry of Miami is grieving, and you stand outside of my company hounding me for the latest juicy gossip, so there it is. The woman you're ripping apart singlehandedly fired off this investigation by not only uncovering the truth but finding the proof behind it. And I happen to be in love with her. I will no longer hide my feelings for this woman, and you will no longer picket my company. If any more personal or professional property destruction should come about because of your inability to follow laws, I will have every single one of you arrested."

Then, without taking any questions, I stepped down from my podium and went down into the parking garage.

I pulled my keys from my pocket and searched for my Jaguar. The lights lit up as I unlocked the doors and slipped into the car. I wasn't staying here another second. I said what I'd come to say, and it was the last time I was saying it. As I pulled out of the parking garage, cops hauled a few more kicking and screaming press away from my building in handcuffs, and a sweet victory rose up my body.

It was time for me to get back to Ashley.

I pulled into a parking space across the road and headed straight for her apartment. The smell Chinese food wafted through the door as I knocked on it. Cassidy opened it up, a huge smile on her face, and when Ashley whipped her head around, she leaped off the couch. She ran to me, and I opened my arms to her, scooping her up against my body.

I walked us both into her apartment as my lips peppered kisses along her cheek.

"I heard it all," she said.

"I know you did."

"Did you mean it?" she asked.

I set her back down onto her feet and cupped her cheek in the palm of my hand.

"Every word of it," I said.

She stood to her toes and pressed her lips against mine, the taste of noodles on her tongue. I cupped the back of her head and held her to me, relishing in the moment before Cassidy cleared her throat.

"You still want your kung pao chicken, Jimmy?"

She dangled the box on the tip of her finger as a grin crossed my cheeks.

"Yes I do," I said. "If I'm allowed to stay?"

"You're always allowed to stay," Ashley said. "Even if I say you can't."

Chapter 24

Ashley

My gut reaction was still not to go back to work, but I needed some semblance of normalcy in my life. Dwelling on my mother's death was doing me no good, and every time I thought about her, the tears started again. I was tired of crying and skulking around. I was tired of forcing Cass away from her business because I couldn't handle the pressure I had ushered into my life of my own accord.

So I got up, got dressed, and headed to work.

I parked across the street to get some coffee but was bombarded by the paparazzi. I slipped into the coffee shop and grabbed a bagel and a large cup, but they were waiting for me when I came out. Cameras were flashing, and microphones were in my face, and I could see the security team from the front of the building trying to get across the busy road.

"Miss Ternbeau, did Jimmy Sheldon force you into this relationship?"

I looked at the reporter like he was insane before I drew a deep breath.

"Absolutely not," I said. "I'm in love with Jimmy Sheldon. He's the best thing that's ever happened to me. I'm sorry if you live the kind of life that feels the need to rip apart something like that."

"So you wanted the relationship, Miss Ternbeau?"

"One hundred percent," I said.

I held my hand up to Jimmy's security team as the reporters continued to bombard me with questions.

"What about Nina Black? Your relationship came on the heels of that one ending? Are you scared you're nothing but a rebound?"

"Jimmy's prior relationship with Miss Black is neither my business nor yours. Now I remember something in Jimmy's press conference yesterday about arrests and such if you guys didn't stop stalking his business and picketing for statements. So I'll give you a chance to get out of here before I call the cops myself."

I stared down the reporter before she snickered and shook her head.

"Privileged bitch."

"Says the woman wearing twelve-hundred-dollar shoes," I said.

The shocked reporter looked down as a smirk drew across my face.

"Just because I don't dress nicely doesn't mean I don't know an expensive pair of shoes when I see them."

The security team was grinning at me as we walked back across the street. Part of me thought this was a bad idea. I'd lost my mother, and surely, they would dig that up somehow, plaster it all over the news and make it a part of some manipulative narrative. I was trying to hold myself together as I walked into the building. Then, I took off in a sprint toward the elevator.

I wanted to get to the safety of my office.

I was running down the hallway when a hand tugged at my arm. I went flying into a room, and the door shut behind me before I looked up to see who it was. It was Jimmy, and his eyes were aflame with something I didn't recognize.

"Should I be in your office right now?" I asked.

"The way you handled yourself out there was incredible," he said. "I'm so proud of you."

"Well, I'm tired of their bullshit. I've had enough of it for a lifetime."

I felt my body breaking down as tears rose to my eyes. Jimmy took my food and coffee from my hands and slid my purse down my arm. He wrapped his grip around me and pulled me close to him. I lost it against him, crying with body-racking sobs as I clung to the jacket of his suit.

"I can't deal with them right now," I said breathlessly.

"And you won't have to any longer. I got their names from the broadcast, and I've contacted their bosses."

"Wait. That was live?" I asked.

"Don't worry about it. You did wonderfully. Ross actually applauded you."

"Ross saw it?"

"Stop. Worrying. Just lean into me."

"It's all too much. It's still too much. Why can't I handle this, Jimmy? Why am I so weak?"

"One, you're not weak. You're far from it. And two, you just lost your mother," he said.

"Oh, Mom."

"I want you to take off until after the funeral."

"I can't do that," I said.

"You can, and you will. You need to. Planning this funeral is going to take every ounce of energy you have, and you should devote it to that and nothing else."

"Ross won't like that," I said.

"Ross doesn't have a say in it. As the owner and operator of this company, I'm telling you to take the time fully and completely off until your mother's funeral is over."

"But it took all this energy to get in here," I said.

"Then I'll help alleviate the energy it takes to get out of here," he said.

I nodded as I picked up my things and Jimmy escorted me back downstairs. He walked me across the street to my car and even held my door open for me. There were still a few journalists on the sidewalk, but I could tell they were wary of approaching. Jimmy was holding fast to his "arrest any journalist in sight" threat, and it was making them fearful of approaching.

Why didn't they simply go away?

I watched Jimmy recede in my rearview mirror as I drove back to my apartment. I went through another box of my mother's things before deciding to go see Cass at her bakery. I'd pulled her away from it enough, and I felt bad for her having to put up with all my bullshit.

So I swung into her favorite wing place and got us some lunch.

"Ashley? I'm shocked to see you in here."

"Wings and girl talk to get my mind off stuff?" I asked.

"I saw that impromptu interview on the television this morning. You owned that shit. You should be proud."

"I'm over all of that media bullshit," I said. "This is a little bit of a thanks from me for keeping my mind off things and putting up with my antics while I was putting up with everyone else's."

"Just a bit? Good. Because it's going to take a lot of wings to make up for that."

"Trust me. I know."

"So what do you want to talk about?"

"Anything other than my mother, Jimmy, work, or the press."

"So ... how's Chipper?" she asked with a grin.

"You're a dick."

"And you're going to be okay."

I watched Cass put her hand on top of mine as I sighed heavily.

"I miss her," I said.

"You will, but if she's not here, that means she's no longer trapped in a body that can't remember the world around her. Now, she's free."

"Why doesn't that bring any comfort?" I asked.

"Because you want your mother. There's nothing wrong with that."

"When will it stop hurting?" I asked. "When will my heart stop feeling like it's being crushed in a vice?"

"When you learn to live your life without her. In some ways, you already know how. Now it's a matter of knowing how to survive without constantly having to worry about her medically and physically."

"I miss the person she used to be. In some ways, I've already grieved over that."

"I figured," she said.

"Does that make me a bad daughter?"

"No. It makes you a practical one. And we all knew your mother. She was nothing if not practical."

"That woman could use reason to get out of any corner you backed her into."

"She was a fighter," Cass said. "All her life. And now? She can relax because she doesn't have to fight her body any longer."

I felt an odd blanket of peace fall over me as those words graced my ears.

"I love you, Cass," I said.

"I love you, too, Ashley."

Chapter 25

Jimmy
One Week Later

After an entire week and having the police arrest and detain over thirty journalists and reporters, the media was finally dying down about my relationship with Ashley. The funeral for her mother had been three days ago, and Ashley had resumed her duties at work. I could tell she was still in a haze, but her simple presence at the board of investors meetings brought peace down on all of them.

They enjoyed having her back, and so did I.

I wanted to take Ashley out on a date, but I was concerned it was too soon. I knew things were still delicate, but I also wanted to take her mind off things she was still thinking about. I could see her zoning out sometimes in her office, staring out over the expanse of Miami or staring blankly at a wall.

I also wanted the chance to privately prove that what I'd said to the press was true.

I wanted her to know I was still there for her during this hard time. Even though the press was dying down and there was no more funeral to plan, I wanted her to know I knew she was still in pain, and I wasn't shying away from that simply because she wasn't approaching me at work.

So I picked up my phone and called her office phone.

"Ashley Ternbeau."

Her voice sounded so empty and defeated.

"How are you feeling?" I asked.

I heard her sniffle, and it broke my heart.

"A lot. That's really all I can say."

"With the media dying down and people leaving us alone, I wanted to ask if you wanted to try the beach house again."

"I don't know, Jimmy."

"A home-cooked meal. The sun setting. A glass of wine. Talking or no talking if that's what you prefer. We could walk along the beach. Or go get another cup of that coffee."

"I've been craving that coffee," she said.

"What do you say? Today, after work? Maybe spend the night? Or the weekend?"

"I don't have any clothes with me," she said.

"Do you have some in your closet?"

"None that are appropriate for the beach."

"Then, we'll stay inside. Watch the beauty from the comfort of my bed," I said.

"That actually sounds nice."

"Come by my office once you're done for the day, and we'll head out," I said.

The day inched on, but it finally drew to a close. Ashley was standing at my door waiting for me with a couple of outfits folded up in her purse. I placed my hand on the small of her back before I locked up my office, and then the two of us headed down to my car.

We drove out to my beach house with the windows rolled down. Ashley's beautiful hair was flying around her face, and she looked relaxed as she closed her eyes. She leaned the seat back and drank in the feel of the salty air on her skin, and I revved the engine for her listening pleasure.

A small grin appeared on her cheeks, and it made my heart hammer against my chest.

We pulled up, and the smells from dinner were already wafting out the windows. Ashley threw me a confused look as I ushered her up the steps. I'd hired a personal chef for the evening, and he was almost done as we walked through the doors.

There were even glasses of wine waiting for us.

"Jimmy. What is all this?" she asked.

"A free night for us to talk or sit in silence and watch the waves roll in," I said.

"Thank you so much," she said.

"Anything for you."

We dropped our stuff on the couch, and I gestured to the chef to bring our food out onto the porch. He served us, and I handed him his check before he cleaned up and left. The food was amazing. Mouthwatering, even. The chicken melted in our mouths, and the vegetables were cooked perfectly. The homemade honey bread was fantastic.

We stuffed ourselves full, leaving no leftovers for us to pack up.

We sat in silence, finishing off the bottle of white wine that had been paired with dinner. We watched the sunset over the ocean, and Ashley seemed a little more okay. She sipped on her wine and relaxed back. She stretched her legs out and crossed them at her ankles. Her body language was very open for everything she had been through, and I debated on whether this was the right time.

There was nothing I could do to take her pain away, but I wanted her to know I was there for her, and I was never going away if she didn't want me to. I stuck my hand in my pocket and fiddled with the small box.

Ashley caught the movement.

"What is that?" she asked.

"What is what?"

"That thing you're playing with. I saw it that day you pulled me into your office before the nursing home called."

I guess it was going to be the right time.

I pulled it out of my pocket and held it between my fingers. I turned the box around, trying to formulate my words as best as I could. Ashley shifted in her seat, her body turned toward me as her eyes looked me up and down.

Then I turned toward her and sat the box on the table.

"I know there's nothing I can do or say to take your pain away, Ashley, but I want you to know that I'm here for you."

"I appreciate that, Jimmy."

Her eyes were locked on the box as I picked it up and opened it. The diamond and the aquamarine stones caught the rest of the setting sun. Ashley gasped when she saw it. I slid it across the table toward her and folded my hands together.

"Jimmy, what is this?" she asked.

"There are no words to describe how happy I am that you let me back in," I said. "When I thought I'd lost you, it ruined a part of me inside. I couldn't get you out of my head, and everywhere I looked I saw something that reminded me of you. You seeped into my veins, Ashley. You imprinted yourself on me in a way no other woman has."

"Oh my gosh," she whispered.

"I love you more than I've loved anyone or anything on this planet. I was ready to burn my company to the ground if it meant keeping you, if it meant getting the press off your back and allowing you to live the quiet life you want."

"Jimmy," she said.

"Will you take a walk with me?" I asked.

Her eyes whipped up to me as I picked up the box and held out my hand.

She took it and allowed me to lead her down to the beach. The last of the sun was guiding our way as I walked her out to a patch of sand. There were rose petals in the shape of a heart, standing directly in front of the last sliver of sun. I got down onto one knee and held the box up, watching as Ashley's hands flew to her lips.

"I know it might be too soon, but the moment I saw this ring, I thought of you. Every time I closed my eyes, I saw this moment. On the beach. With the sun. And with you. I want to marry you, Ashley Ternbeau. I want to live the rest of my life burning everything to the ground as long as it makes you happy. I want you to have everything you could possibly want, and I never want you to wonder if you'll ever be alone. Because you won't be. I won't allow it. I want to run this company with you, but more than that, I want to run this life with you. We don't have to get married anytime soon, but Ashley, will you marry me?"

Tears were streaming down her cheeks as she knelt in front of me. Her hands smoothed up my chest to wrap around my neck. Her eyes reflected the moon and the stars as the sun turned its lights off in the distance, and as she pressed her lips into mine, I felt her answer.

"Yes," she said into my lips. "I will marry you."

Chapter 26

Ashley

Passion overcame me, and I pulled Jimmy down to the sand. The white sheet he had laid out for the rose petals caught our fall, and my legs spread for him. The ocean was lapping at our toes as his hands meandered along my body, and I felt his hand slide that beautiful ring onto my finger.

"I love you," I said breathlessly. "So much, Jimmy."

The nighttime blanketed our naked bodies when he finally pressed his cock deep into my pussy. I arched into his hands massaging my breasts. My fingertips curled into his back, tracing his strength as he rolled his hips against mine. We shared our air and whispered promises of endless love as our bodies moved as one.

The ocean was coming up to our knees, washing a few of the petals away. The sheet was soaking up the saltwater as Jimmy pulled me to his body. He sat us up, his arms wrapped around me, and my face fell into the crook of his neck. I nipped at his skin and kissed up to his cheek as his cock throbbed against my walls.

"I love you. Thank you. For coming back to me."

Jimmy's words were hot in my ear as I ground onto his dick. I rolled deeply into him, my knees soaked by the ocean as it ran along our skin. My toes curled, and the world beginning to dip as Jimmy thrust up into my body.

His hands fell to my hips, and we lost ourselves in one another. Sweat dripped down my chest, and sweat was falling off his brow. I placed sloppy kisses against his skin as I rode his cock, feeling that burning sensation in the pit of my gut as his hands cupped my ass. He rolled me into him, stroking my clit and filling my pussy. He grew thicker and thicker, pulling moans and groans from my throat. The ocean was beating against our bodies, covering us from the world as we grunted and cried out.

My body leaned back as Jimmy's hands held steady around me.

My legs shook, and my pussy clamped down as his cock stilled within my body. My jaw unhinged as the moonlight bathed my naked skin in the little bit of warmth it could provide. Jimmy pressed his face into my tits, kissing and biting and sucking at my nipples, rolling my orgasm into another one as his name tumbled from my lips.

"Jimmy. Jimmy. Jimmy, yes. Don't stop. Oh, fuck. Jimmy."

He moaned into my skin as his cock filled me with his come. Thread after thread. Pump after pump. I fell forward, my lips falling into his as he held me tightly.

I could feel him quaking against me, his own orgasm leaving him breathless.

I curled into him, basking in his arms wrapped around me. When his legs finally stopped shaking, he turned us around in the water and stood up. His cock still filling my pussy and my legs and arms wrapped around him, he walked us out into the ocean until the waves were no longer smacking us, and the moon was reflected on top of the water.

I stared at my ring as Jimmy slowly moved my body up and down his thickening cock as the waves slowly buoyed us around. I pressed my lips to his. My hands traveled along his muscles, feeling them twitch as he slowly fucked his cock with my body.

"I love you so much," I said.

"You're the best thing that's ever happened to me," he said.

"This ring, it's beaut—"

My clit brushed against him just right, and it caused me to gasp.

"Not as 'beaut' as you are," he said with a grin.

"Shut up," I said as my forehead rested against his.

"Never."

"Figured it was worth a shot," I said breathlessly.

Our bodies slowly warmed up until we were creating our own waves. I clung to him, allowing him the control and the dominance as he bounced my body. My heels pressed into his back and my nails dug into his shoulders. The ring was sparkling, my lips were moaning, and my eyes were screwed shut.

And I could hear Jimmy grunting in my ear.

Our bodies stilled one last time as pleasure raced over my body. I pulled him closer than I ever had before and locked my legs around him. His cock slid farther and farther into my body as my pussy took his whole length, pulling him deeper and milking him for anything he had left to give.

Jimmy trembled as he gave our weight away to the ocean, allowing the water to support us as we floated along in the ocean.

"We don't have to plan the wedding right away," he said.

"I know you're worried about that," I said. "Don't worry. It was the perfect time."

I watched his eyes light up before he drew me in for a kiss. I could feel him slowly pull out of me, our juices leaking into the ocean, washing away from our bodies as we clung to one another in the water. Like a renewal of the life we were going to live together.

"Planning a wedding would help me get my mind off things," I said.

"It would?" Jimmy asked.

"Mhm. It would also give me something to be hopeful about after all of this ... stuff."

"This stuff."

"Uh-huh. I could bury myself into planning a beautiful wedding for us, and in a way, the starting of our new life could help me cope with the ashes of my old one."

"I would say that's a touch dramatic, but given these past few months, it sounds like a perfect explanation."

"Especially since you said you were willing to burn your company down for me—which I wouldn't let you do, by the way."

"But I would've been willing to do it if it helped you," he said.

"You thanked me for letting you back in, but I didn't thank you for the same."

"If it's any consolation, my legs are still weak. So that can be your thank-you."

"You're insane, you know that?"

"You're the one who has me all twisted up inside. Not my fault," he said with a grin.

"At any rate, thank you, Jimmy, for letting me back into your life and your company."

"We need you, Ashley. I need you."

"And I need you," I said.

Our lips connected in a small, sensual kiss before Jimmy's legs started to kick. The current had carried us downstream from our clothes, and it was going to take us a little while to get back to them. We swam for the shore, splashing one another and dunking the other in the ocean. Belly laughter rose up my throat and fell from my lips, starting the erasure of the tears and the nightmares I'd been living with for the past couple of weeks.

We scrambled to our clothes and pulled them back on before we ran up the steps to the beach house.

Jimmy swung me around in his arms before the two of us went back inside. We left our dirty dishes on the porch, resolving ourselves to a hot shower. We tossed our clothes into the hamper and stepped in, ready to wash the sand off our bodies.

Instead, I found my back pinned against the shower wall.

I moaned and cried out and chanted his name. My toes curled so hard, they cramped my legs. The hot water rushed over our orgasming bodies, and Jimmy's lips couldn't leave my skin. It was like they were magnetized to me.

We washed ourselves up and collapsed into bed, water dripping from our limbs. I curled up underneath the covers with him and placed my head on his chest. His finger was circling the ring around my hand, twisting it and turning it as our bodies dried against the bed.

This was the life I wanted with him. Not his money or his company or lavish trips or expensive cars. I wanted the quiet moments in the most desolate of times. I wanted the moments when I knew he would be there no matter what. I wanted the random passionate moments when he couldn't keep his hands off me and the moments when we lay in bed satisfied with the silence.

I wanted all the things people considered fillers, and I wanted him to be present in all of it.

"Pale blue and green," I said.

"Hmm?" Jimmy asked.

"The colors for our wedding. Pale blue and green."

"Whatever you want," he said as he stroked my back. "Whatever you want, my love."

Epilogue

Jimmy
One Year Later

As I stood waiting for the wedding to begin, I reflected on the past year, the ups and down Ashley and I had faced. The trial had come after Markus was successfully captured trying to declare bankruptcy in Florida. Less than twenty-four hours afterward, Markus had been sentenced to twelve years in prison, and I was about to become the luckiest man on the face of the planet. Funny how things worked out.

He should have gotten one hundred and twenty years, given the amount of money he stole from multiple companies. But I caved. I spoke up for him and attested to the man I knew. Ashley didn't like it, and neither did my lawyer, but a fifty-four-year-old man in jail for twelve years would take away the rest of the prime of his life. Markus would come out at the age of sixty-six with nothing to his name, no business to manage, and no one who would trust him.

Except Nina, of course.

The biggest shocker came a few days before the trial. Even though Nina had successfully moved to California to begin her life over, a new link was uncovered, a link that made everything fall into place. Nina had been working with Markus.

Not only that, but the two of them had been lovers. Intensely engulfed in a sordid affair while Markus swindled multiple companies. She was the beauty behind the operation, and he was the brains. Markus's girlfriend, Jamie, had been one of Nina's good friends sent there as a trap to throw every single one of us off. The social media scandal? Orchestrated by Markus with Nina willingly set up to take the fall if necessary. The attempted burning of my files room? Nina's divine plan with the help of Markus's money. When Nina and I had argued and she yelled at me that she didn't need my money, she was very serious because she was living off Markus and his fortune.

That was how the rest of Markus's assets had been seized. Once we found the link between him and Nina, the rest of his properties and accounts surfaced in her name. She had been draining me of money during our arrangement to get close to me, to delve deeper into my company. Her antics at the dinner that ultimately spiraled toward our demise? Orchestrated by her to set things in motion for Markus.

It made me so sick to find out, I physically threw up.

Through it all, Ashley had been there, not only professionally but personally. My lawyer begged me to press charges against Nina, but I didn't. Between removing the lifestyle she was used to and putting her beau beyond bars, that was enough torture for her. She would live in California with nothing to her name and no work experience to garner her anything close to what she was used to.

To me, that was enough punishment for a woman like her.

Of course, Markus was staying positive through it all. He was intent on getting out of jail early on good behavior, but my lawyer kept reassuring me it wouldn't happen. He was a confident son of a bitch, and every once in a while, he would try to call, but I ignored all his calls.

I eventually changed my number so he couldn't contact me any longer.

I owed Ashley my life. I owed her my company. Because of the errors she'd caught and pursued, my company was still standing with its dignity intact. My stubbornness almost lost me everything, but her forgiving soul allowed me a second chance at the life I saw with her.

I wasn't going to take that for granted.

All in all, I was awarded a settlement that covered what was stolen plus a lot more. We were only seeing it in chunks as his assets were broken down and sold off, but it made the investors happy, so happy, in fact, they were investing the most they'd ever given Big Steps in its entire lifespan.

After all the drama and all the heartache, my company was in a better place than when all this shit started.

The string quartet I'd hired for the wedding ceremony struck up their tune. Their toes were sunken into the sand in front of my beach house as the ocean ebbed against the shoreline. Ashley wanted to have a small beach wedding consisting only of those we loved and trusted and cherished. I watched as Cassidy, Ashley's maid of honor, walked down the rose petal walkway. Her pale blue dress was blowing in the breeze as Ross, my best man, escorted her down the aisle.

But my eyes were trained behind them on the beautiful woman walking down the steps.

As I stood with Ross beside me, I watched Ashley come down the steps. She wore a simple white dress that blew around her legs with the wind. The lacey bodice was strapless and clung to her curves in ways I couldn't describe. The green clip in her hair securing her veil matched her twinkling eyes. Her gaze locked on mine, and her hair blew in the breeze, whipping around the beautiful face I'd wake up to every morning for the rest of my life. She was breathtaking.

I was the luckiest man on the planet.

Bernie stood in front of us with a Bible in his hand. He coached us into the vows we had written for one another as we exchanged rings and vows filled with love and devotion. I promised to always protect Ashley. To keep her warm, to keep her fed, and to keep her at my side no matter what. I promised to always trust her opinion, take into account her beliefs, and to always make sure her morals were never compromised when living her life alongside mine. And in the end, Ashley promised to always be open, to communicate, and to be brave enough to lean on me while we spent our lives loving each other. We slid our rings on each other reverently before I pressed my lips against the lips of my wife. Patrice was standing by the string quartet, clapping and cheering us on as I dipped Ashley back. I kissed her fiercely, reminding her of the passion she would experience for the rest of her days.

The ceremony was small, but the reception was decadent. It was held at the same hotel Ashley and I had met at over a year ago. The entire company was invited to dance and eat and celebrate with us, with Bernie and Patrice offering to provide their wonderful coffee as well as a menu of their mouthwatering foods. I twirled Ashley around and held her against my body, dancing with her as if we were the only two in the room.

Then, Ross got up to the microphone and cleared his throat.

"Excuse me? Is this thing on?"

The dancing stopped as everyone turned to look at Ross on the stage.

"Yes. Hello. Hi, everyone. Are we all having a good time?"

People clapped and cheered as I pressed a kiss to Ashley's cheek.

"Good. I just have a few words. Then we'll get back to the dancing."

"After I say something!" Cassidy said.

"After Miss Cassidy speaks," Ross said. "I've known Jimmy for most of my adult life. Throughout those years, I came to understand two basic truths about him. One, the man knows how to throw a party."

Everyone burst into cheers again as Ashley giggled at my side.

"And two, he is fiercely dedicated to anything that captures his heart. And Ashley? You have most certainly captured his heart. In Jimmy, you don't simply have a husband. You have a life partner. A biggest fan. A very, very loud cheerleader. But the thing that makes you guys work is that you provide him with the same. You don't try to change one another, but you do aspire to make each other better. That takes teamwork, and that's how I know you two will last. To Jimmy and Ashley!"

"To Jimmy and Ashley," everyone said.

"Okay, okay, okay. Now it's my turn," Cassidy said.

I shook my head and pulled Ashley close as her best friend took the microphone from mine.

"I'll make this short and sweet," she said. "Ashley, you're my girl, and you know I've always got your back. But Jimmy is literally the only person who has ever come into your life that I've had the pleasure of defending. He's not just a good man, but he's good for you. As your best friend—and I say this from the bottom of my heart—I won't let you screw it up. I like having a rich guy in the family. Makes things fun."

The crowd chuckled as Ashley leaned her head against my body.

"But on a serious note, I really am happy for you, Ash. I've known you for years, and I've never known you to latch onto someone the way you have Jimmy. Cling to him, even when you don't want to look at him. Love him, even when you can't stand him. Let him be close to you, even when you want room to breathe. Because it's in those moments when you're reminded of this one, when you know you're making the right decision in choosing him. To Jimmy and Ashley."

"To Jimmy and Ashley," everyone said.

The party continued, but I whisked my lovely bride away. I scooped her up into my arms and walked her to the elevator. Then, the two of us rode to the very top, to the penthouse suite that had started it all.

Only this time, it was preparing us for our honeymoon.

"Are you excited about tomorrow?" I asked.

"How could I not be? A month-long exploration of Europe, Jimmy. You went too far with that."

"Nothing's too far for my wife," I said with a grin. "You've never been to Europe, so I wanted to take you."

"But a month?"

"Do you not like it?"

"I love it. I don't want you missing too much work," she said.

"Don't worry. I ran it by the boss. He's good with it."

The giggle that fell from her lips fluttered my heart against my chest.

"I still can't believe we're married," she said.

"I can. I'm the happiest I've ever been, and it's only going to get better from here."

"Funny. I was thinking the exact same thing."

I smiled down at the wondrous woman in my arms as the elevator doors opened.

A chilled bottle of champagne and two delicate flutes greeted us along with alcohol-soaked and chocolate-dipped fruits. I carried Ashley over the threshold and then sat her down on her feet. I walked over and grabbed the bottle, hoisting it out of the ice before I unscrewed the metal from the cork.

Then, I aimed it at the wall and popped it open.

Ashley squealed with delight as I poured us each a glass. I set the bottle back into the ice, my eyes dancing over the beauty of my bride. The flush of her cheeks. The tint of her lips. The makeup of her gorgeous green eyes and the rolling valleys of her curves. I handed her a glass, and our fingertips connected, sending electricity shooting up my arm.

"To love, to life, and to Europe," I said.

"To the rest of our lives," Ashley said.

We clinked our glasses together before our eyes connected. Her lips curled around the edge of the glass as the liquid disappeared between those beautiful lips. I plucked her glass from between her fingertips and wrapped my arm around her, drawing her close to me. I could smell the alcohol on her breath as she picked up a strawberry, holding it to my lips for me to bite.

Then, she bit down on the other end of it, delivering the sweetest kiss before we enjoyed our chocolate-dipped treasure.

"This suite holds some memories," Ashley said.

"One in particular I seem to remember very clearly," I said.

"Would you have changed anything about that night?" she asked.

"About the way we met?"

I walked her body all the way back into the windows, pressing her hips into them as my lips dipped to her neck.

"No," I said. "And you want to know why?"

I kissed up her neck, listening as gasps fell from her lips.

"Why?" she asked in a whisper.

"Because it brought me to this moment. Changing anything about how we met might sacrifice you, which is something I'll never be willing to do."

Her hands reached up to cup my cheeks as my lips descended to hers. I took her hands and pressed them into the glass, spreading her body out like I had that night. Our kiss turned to nibbles, and my nibbles turned to love bites. Soon, I was tearing her delicate wedding dress from her body and pressing her naked body against the full-length windows.

"Jimmy. I love you. So much."

I rolled my hips into her growing wetness as my nose nuzzled against hers.

"And I love you. Always, and forever."

THE END

Building Billions

Part 1
Part 2
Part 3

Find Lexy Timms:

LEXY TIMMS NEWSLETTER:
http://eepurl.com/9i0vD
Lexy Timms Facebook Page:
https://www.facebook.com/SavingForever
Lexy Timms Website:
http://www.lexytimms.com

Want

FREE READS?

Sign up for Lexy Timms' newsletter
And she'll send you
A paid read, for FREE!

Sign up for news and updates!
http://eepurl.com/9i0vD

More by Lexy Timms:

FROM BEST SELLING AUTHOR, Lexy Timms, comes a billionaire romance that'll make you swoon and fall in love all over again.

Jamie Connors has given up on men. Despite being smart, pretty, and just slightly overweight, she's a magnet for the kind of guys that don't stay around.

Her sister's wedding is at the foreground of the family's attention. Jamie would be find with it if her sister wasn't pressuring her to lose weight so she'll fit in the maid of honor dress, her mother would get off her case and her ex-boyfriend wasn't about to become her brother-in-law.

Determined to step out on her own, she accepts a PA position from billionaire Alex Reid. The job includes an apartment on his property and gets her out of living in her parent's basement.

Jamie has to balance her life and somehow figure out how to manage her billionaire boss, without falling in love with him.

** The Boss is book 1 in the Managing the Bosses series. All your questions won't be answered in the first book. It may end on a cliff hanger.

For mature audiences only. There are adult situations, but this is a love story, NOT erotica.

FRAGILE TOUCH

"HIS BODY IS PERFECT. He's got this face that isn't just heart-melting but actually kind of exotic..."

Lillian Warren's life is just how she's designed it. She has a high-paying job working with celebrities and the elite, teaching them how to better organize their lives. She's on her own, the days quiet, but she likes it that way. Especially since she's still figuring out how to live with her recent diagnosis of Crohn's disease. Her cats keep her company, and she's not the least bit lonely.

Fun-loving personal trainer, Cayden, thinks his neighbor is a killjoy. He's only seen her a few times, and the woman looks like she needs a drink or three. He knows how to party and decides to invite her to over—if he can find her. What better way to impress her than take care of her overgrown yard? She proceeds to thank him by throwing up in his painstakingly-trimmed-to-perfection bushes.

Something about the fragile, mysterious woman captivates him.

Something about this rough-on-the-outside bear of a man attracts Lily, despite her heart warning her to tread carefully.

BUILDING BILLIONS - PART 3

Faking It Description:

HE GROANED. THIS WAS torture. Being trapped in a room with a beautiful woman was just about every man's fantasy, but he had to remember that this was just pretend.

Allyson Smith has crushed on her boss for years, but never dared to make a move. When she finds herself without a date to her brother's upcoming wedding, Allyson tells her family one innocent white lie: that she's been dating her boss. Unfortunately, her boss discovers her lie, and insists on posing as her boyfriend to escort her to the wedding.

Playboy billionaire Dane Prescott always has a new heiress on his arm, but he can't get his assistant Allyson out of his head. He's fought his attraction to her, until he gets caught up in her scheme of a fake relationship.

One passionate weekend with the boss has Allyson Smith questioning everything she believes in. Falling for a wealthy playboy like Dane is against the rules, but if she's just faking it what's the harm?

Capturing Her Beauty

KAYLA REID HAS ALWAYS been into fashion and everything to do with it. Growing up wasn't easy for her. A bigger girl trying to squeeze into the fashion world is like trying to suck an entire gelatin mold through a straw; possible, but difficult.

She found herself an open door as a designer and jumped right in. Her designs always made the models smile. The colors, the fabrics, the styles. Never once did she dream of being on the other side of the lens. She got to watch her clothing strut around on others and that was good enough.

But who says you can't have a little fun when you're off the clock?

Sometimes trying on the latest fashions is just as good as making them. Kayla's hours in front of the mirror were a guilty pleasure.

A chance meeting with one of the company photographers may turn into more than just an impromptu photo shoot.

Hot n' Handsome, Rich & Single... how far are you willing to go?
MEET ALEX REID, CEO of Reid Enterprise. Billionaire extra ordinaire, chiseled to perfection, panty-melter and currently single.

Learn about Alex Reid before he began Managing the Bosses. Alex Reid sits down for an interview with R&S.

His life style is like his handsome looks: hard, fast, breath-taking and out to play ball. He's risky, charming and determined.

How close to the edge is Alex willing to go? Will he stop at nothing to get what he wants?

Alex Reid is book 1 in the R&S Rich and Single Series. Fall in love with these hot and steamy men; all single, successful, and searching for love.

Book One is FREE!
SOMETIMES THE HEART needs a different kind of saving... find out if Charity Thompson will find a way of saving forever in this hospital setting Best-Selling Romance by Lexy Timms

Charity Thompson wants to save the world, one hospital at a time. Instead of finishing med school to become a doctor, she chooses a different path and raises money for hospitals – new wings, equipment, whatever they need. Except there is one hospital she would be happy to never set foot in again—her fathers. So of course he hires her to create a gala for his sixty-fifth birthday. Charity can't say no. Now she is working in the one place she doesn't want to be. Except she's attracted to Dr. Elijah Bennet, the handsome playboy chief.

Will she ever prove to her father that's she's more than a med school dropout? Or will her attraction to Elijah keep her from repairing the one thing she desperately wants to fix?

HEART OF THE BATTLE Series
In a world plagued with darkness, she would be his salvation.

No one gave Erik a choice as to whether he would fight or not. Duty to the crown belonged to him, his father's legacy remaining beyond the grave.

Taken by the beauty of the countryside surrounding her, Linzi would do anything to protect her father's land. Britain is under attack and Scotland is next. At a time she should be focused on suitors, the men of her country have gone to war and she's left to stand alone.

Love will become available, but will passion at the touch of the enemy unravel her strong hold first?

THE RECRUITING TRIP

Aspiring college athlete Aileen Nessa is finding the recruiting process beyond daunting. Being ranked #10 in the world for the 100m hurdles at the age of eighteen is not a fluke, even though she believes that one race, where everything clinked magically together, might be. American universities don't seem to think so. Letters are pouring in from all over the country.

As she faces the challenge of differentiating between a college's genuine commitment to her or just empty promises from talent-seeking coaches, Aileen heads to the University of Gatica, a Division One school, on a recruiting trip. Her best friend dares who to go just to see the cute guys on the school's brochure.

The university's athletic program boasts one of the top hurdlers in the country. Tyler Jensen is the school's NCAA champion in the hurdles and Jim Thorpe recipient for top defensive back in football. His incredible blue-green eyes, confident smile and rock hard six pack abs mess with Aileen's concentration.

His offer to take her under his wing, should she choose to come to Gatica, is a temping proposition that has her wondering if she might be with an angel or making a deal with the devil himself.

THE ONE YOU CAN'T FORGET

Emily Rose Dougherty is a good Catholic girl from mythical Walkerville, CT. She had somehow managed to get herself into a heap trouble with the law, all because an ex-boyfriend has decided to make things difficult.

Luke "Spade" Wade owns a Motorcycle repair shop and is the Road Captain for Hades' Spawn MC. He's shocked when he reads in the paper that his old high school flame has been arrested. She's always been the one he couldn't forget.

Will destiny let them find each other again? Or what happens in the past, best left for the history books?

*** This is book 1 of the Hades' Spawn MC Series. All your questions may not be answered in the first book.*

LEXY TIMMS
CONFESSION OF A
Tattooist
Lexy
Timms
Grab Your
FREE
Copy Today!

FORTUNE RIDERS INC
BILLIONAIRE BIKER
LEXY TIMMS
Download For
FREE
Lexy
Timms

HOUSE ROMANCE
CAUGHT
FLAMES
BESTSELLING AUTHOR
LEXY TIMMS
LIMITED TIME
Lexy Timms
FREE
DOWNLOAD

ONE YOU CAN'T
Forget
BESTSELLING AUTHOR
LEXY TIMMS
Lexy Timms
Grab Your
FREE
Copy Today!

Lexy
Timms
THE
BOSS
Managing the Bosses: Book 1
Lexy
Timms
Grab your
copy today!

Lexy
Timms
FOREVER
FOREVER
FOREVER
BOOK 3
BOOK 2
BOOK 1
Saving
FOREVER
Lexy
Timms
Limited
Time for
99cents

LEXY TIMMS
BEATING THE

LEXY TIMMS
MOMENT IN TIME: BOOK ONE
HIGHLANDERS
Bride

Don't miss out!

Click the button below and you can sign up to receive emails whenever Lexy Timms publishes a new book. There's no charge and no obligation.

https://books2read.com/r/B-A-NNL-IOFS

BOOKS 2 READ

Connecting independent readers to independent writers.

Did you love *Building Billions - Part 3*? Then you should read *Rhyme* by Lexy Timms!

Music is what feelings sound like.

Olivia Dane, a hard-working lawyer, has just been dumped by her fiancée. To make matters worse, he did it via text message. Deciding to drown her sorrows at a local pub, Olivia is intent on forgetting about men altogether. Instead, she's going to focus on her career, and if she plays her cards right, she might just make partner at her firm.

It isn't long before her plans are completely derailed by an irresistibly sexy stranger who guides her to a dark corner of the bar. This gorgeous alpha male isn't your ordinary man. It's Logan Graham, lead guitarist of the insanely popular Scottish rock band. A man used to getting anything he wants, whenever he wants it.

What starts out as a wildly passionate one-night-stand quickly turns into a far more complicated relationship when the curvy lawyer discovers that the bad-boy rocker is her newest client. To make matters worse if she doesn't win the case he'll lose everything he's worked so hard for.

And there's even more trouble on the horizon when Olivia boss discovers her new relationship and threatens to destroy her career if she doesn't give him the one thing he's always wanted - her.

Warning: *This is a steamy romance story that includes adult content suitable for readers 18+*

Hard Rocked Series:
Rhyme
Harmony
Lyrics

Also by Lexy Timms

A Chance at Forever Series
Forever Perfect
Forever Desired
Forever Together

Alpha Bad Boy Motorcycle Club Triology
Alpha Biker
Alpha Revenge
Alpha Outlaw
Alpha Purpose

BBW Romance Series
Capturing Her Beauty
Pursuing Her Dreams
Tracing Her Curves

Beating the Biker Series
Making Her His

Making the Break
Making of Them

Billionaire Holiday Romance Series
Driving Home for Christmas
The Valentine Getaway
Cruising Love

Billionaire in Disguise Series
Facade
Illusion
Charade

Billionaire Secrets Series
The Secret
Freedom
Courage
Trust

Building Billions
Building Billions - Part 1
Building Billions - Part 2
Building Billions - Part 3

Conquering Warrior Series
Ruthless

Diamond in the Rough Anthology
Billionaire Rock
Billionaire Rock - part 2

Dominating PA Series
Her Personal Assistant - Part 1
Her Personal Assistant Box Set

Fake Billionaire Series
Faking It
Temporary CEO
Caught in the Act
Never Tell A Lie
Fake Christmas

Firehouse Romance Series
Caught in Flames
Burning With Desire
Craving the Heat
Firehouse Romance Complete Collection

Fortune Riders MC Series
Billionaire Biker
Billionaire Ransom
Billionaire Misery

Fragile Series
Fragile Touch
Fragile Kiss
Fragile Love

Hades' Spawn Motorcycle Club
One You Can't Forget
One That Got Away
One That Came Back
One You Never Leave
One Christmas Night
Hades' Spawn MC Complete Series

Hard Rocked Series
Rhyme

Heart of Stone Series
The Protector
The Guardian

The Warrior

Heart of the Battle Series
Celtic Viking
Celtic Rune
Celtic Mann
Heart of the Battle Series Box Set

Heistdom Series
Master Thief

Just About Series
About Love
About Truth
About Forever

Love You Series
Love Life
Need Love
My Love

Managing the Bosses Series
The Boss
The Boss Too

Who's the Boss Now
Love the Boss
I Do the Boss
Wife to the Boss
Employed by the Boss
Brother to the Boss
Senior Advisor to the Boss
Forever the Boss
Christmas With the Boss
Gift for the Boss - Novella 3.5

Moment in Time
Highlander's Bride
Victorian Bride
Modern Day Bride
A Royal Bride
Forever the Bride

Outside the Octagon
Submit

Reverse Harem Series
Primals

RIP Series
Track the Ripper

Hunt the Ripper
Pursue the Ripper

R&S Rich and Single Series
Alex Reid
Parker

Saving Forever
Saving Forever - Part 1
Saving Forever - Part 2
Saving Forever - Part 3
Saving Forever - Part 4
Saving Forever - Part 5
Saving Forever - Part 6
Saving Forever Part 7
Saving Forever - Part 8
Saving Forever Boxset Books #1-3

Shifting Desires Series
Jungle Heat

Southern Romance Series
Little Love Affair
Siege of the Heart
Freedom Forever
Soldier's Fortune

Tattooist Series
Confession of a Tattooist
Surrender of a Tattooist
Heart of a Tattooist
Hopes & Dreams of a Tattooist

Tennessee Romance
Whisky Lullaby
Whisky Melody
Whisky Harmony

The Brush Of Love Series
Every Night
Every Day
Every Time
Every Way
Every Touch

The Debt
The Debt: Part 1 - Damn Horse
The Debt: Complete Collection

The University of Gatica Series
The Recruiting Trip

Faster
Higher
Stronger
Dominate
No Rush
University of Gatica - The Complete Series

T.N.T. Series
Troubled Nate Thomas - Part 1
Troubled Nate Thomas - Part 2
Troubled Nate Thomas - Part 3

Undercover Series
Perfect For Me
Perfect For You
Perfect For Us

Unknown Identity Series
Unknown
Unpublished
Unexposed
Unsure
Unwritten
Unknown Identity Box Set: Books #1-3

Unlucky Series

Unlucky in Love
UnWanted
UnLoved Forever

Standalone
Wash
Loving Charity
Summer Lovin'
Love & College
Billionaire Heart
First Love
Frisky and Fun Romance Box Collection
Managing the Bosses Box Set #1-3

Printed in Dunstable, United Kingdom